D1539088

SECRETS OF
WAYFARERS INN

The Secret Ingredient

JANICE THOMPSON

Guideposts

New York

SECRETS OF
WAYFARERS INN

The Secret Ingredient

To Peyton, my little mini-me: Writer,
baker, mischief-maker. Nina loves you!

Then Jesus declared, "I am the bread of life.
Whoever comes to me will never go hungry,
and whoever believes in me will never be thirsty."
—John 6:35 NIV

CHAPTER ONE

G o, Winnie! You've got this!" Janice Eastman's voice rang
out above the crowd of onlookers at Washington County's
Rising Star Baking Competition. "You're the best!"

Embarrassed at her sudden outburst, she put a hand over
her mouth and then pulled it away to speak to her friends
standing nearby. "I can't believe I just did that. Must be the
heat getting to me." Or maybe it had more to do with the
excitement of the day. Rooting for a good friend at a large competition like this was all new to her.

"It was a little out of character for you, Janice." Tess Wallace
wiped the moisture from her brow with the back of her hand.
"But I'll agree about the heat. It's really getting to me too. And
the humidity's not helping."

"Why anyone would choose to hold a baking contest outside
during the month of August is beyond me." LuAnn Sherrill
fanned herself with a program and strained to see around the
woman in front of them who was wearing a pink wide-brimmed
hat. "Can you even imagine how hot it is on that stage, what
with all the cameras and ovens and lights? I'm surprised they
haven't had to call 911 for any of the competitors yet."

Janice nodded and lifted the hair off her neck in an attempt
to cool herself down.

LuAnn fanned herself with her hand. "Where is Robin with those water bottles?"

Tess leaned to the right to see through the crowd. "She left ages ago. I hope she didn't get distracted at the cake booth. I saw the most delicious-looking German chocolate cake over there with coconut-pecan icing. I can almost taste it now."

Janice could almost taste it too, but she had more important things to think about right now. "Focus, ladies. We're here to support Winnie, not add more carbs to our diet."

"Speak for yourself." Tess chuckled and licked her lips.

Janice turned her attention to the stage where several tables were arranged in perfect rows, giving the audience an excellent view of the individual competitors. Each baker had her own station, equipped with a stove, table, ingredients, mixer, and utensils. Winnie Washington, Janice's close friend and the inn's renowned cook, looked up from her station and offered a confident smile.

"She must be feeling pretty good about how things are going." Janice's gaze shifted to the large banner featuring the colors of the Rising Star Flour logo. It hung over the stage, advertising the event with great fanfare. Every now and again a hint of a breeze caught the edge of it, causing the deep blue and orange letters to ripple ever so slightly.

The emcee—a short, jolly man representing the company—made his way from station to station, microphone in hand, interviewing the participants. Not that any of them looked particularly thrilled with the interruption. Like Winnie, they seemed pretty focused, including one blonde in four-inch heels. Janice didn't recognize the woman, but she was very well put together, if such a thing could be judged from her hot-pink and lime-green apron.

"Winnie's hanging in there, like it's not fazing her at all," LuAnn chimed in. "And don't be embarrassed about cheering for her, Janice. You're proud of her. We all are."

"If anyone can pull off a win, Winnie can." Tess laughed. "It's even in her name."

"Winnie's already a winner in my book," LuAnn said. "And I'm not just being punny."

Janice laughed at her friends' remarks and then turned her attention back to the stage. Winnie seemed to have things well in hand. She peeked in the oven and gave a thumbs-up, signifying that her pie was nearly done.

"How much longer do you think it will be?" Tess asked.

LuAnn glanced at her watch. "Ten minutes until the buzzer goes off for the pie baking competition. I'm still tickled pink that she won the bread category. Since she came in second in the cake category, if she wins this one, she'll go on to the state finals."

"She'll win this round," Janice said confidently. "No one makes a better pie than Winnie."

Tess fussed with her hair, which had gotten a little fuzzy in the extreme humidity. "I agree. And I'm just glad this day has come at last. I've put on four pounds since she started trying out all her entries on us in preparation."

Robin arrived carrying four bottles of water. "You wouldn't believe how much I paid for these." She passed one in Janice's direction. "It's absurd what they charge for a bottle of water these days."

LuAnn took a sip, then sealed the cap and held it against the back of her neck. "There. That should help cool me down. I hope I don't faint."

"I don't know how Winnie is holding up under this heat. I'm glad she has Georgia in the wings in case she needs something." Janice waved at the petite young woman, but Winnie's assistant was too busy watching Winnie's every move to notice. Oh, well. "For someone who was a total stranger to us just a few days ago, she seems to fit right in."

"Agreed." Tess nodded. "I like her. She's a real sweetheart. Fun to have around the kitchen."

"Yes, and she's proving to be quite the baker," LuAnn added. "I'm so glad she asked Winnie to mentor her before she heads back to college. It's going to be a shame to lose her at the end of the month."

"I agree. And I'm grateful to Winnie for giving her a place to stay while she's here." Janice's gaze shifted to a man with a notepad and pen in his hands. He moved from competitor to competitor, asking questions and jotting down notes. "I don't think I know that guy." Janice pointed at the tall, thin man— probably in his late twenties—with a balding head. "The one taking notes and pictures. Looks like a pretty expensive camera he's got hanging around his neck."

LuAnn craned her neck to see the guy. "Oh, that's Hank Clive. He works for the *Marietta Times*. Brad told me he just took over for one of their beat reporters. I think he said he's from Kentucky, maybe? Something like that." She seemed to be preoccupied with the contestant in the pink and lime-green apron. "Do either of you know that woman? The one who won the cake round?"

"Sandie Ballard." Robin took another swig of her water and held her little battery-powered fan up to her face. "She just opened a bakery a few blocks from the inn. I can't believe you haven't heard. Everyone in town is talking about it. They even did a spot on the radio about it. It's called the Better Batter."

"The Better Batter?" Janice pondered the name. "No wonder she won."

"Trust me when I say everyone's talking about her." Robin released a loud sigh. "I've heard her shop is adorable. Do you think we'll lose customers to her?"

"Nah. What's she got that we haven't got?" Tess asked.

All the ladies turned to gaze at the woman who looked like something straight out of a magazine.

"I can think of about thirty things, but I don't have time to make a list right now." Janice sighed. "Anyway, we'll keep doing what we do, and she can do whatever it is that she does."

At that very moment, a resounding laugh reverberated across the crowd as Sandie chatted with one of the judges.

On the stage, Winnie opened her oven and pulled out her pie. Although too far away to see for sure, Janice thought it looked fine, just the right shade of golden. Before long, the other contestants had their pies out of the oven as well.

Minutes later, the countdown buzzer went off. The contestants filed off the stage and entered the community building where they would wait while their pies cooled or were placed in the blast chiller. The spectators, including the Inn Crowd, were entertained by a local artisan bread maker who demonstrated her techniques and then passed around samples she had prepared earlier.

Then the contestants trooped back to the stage, and the judges made their rounds to sample their pies. Janice whispered a prayer when they got to Winnie. Judging from the look of sheer bliss on a judge's face, she had this one in the bag.

When the judges finished their work, the emcee called all the participants to join him center stage in a long line. He started with third place, which went to an elderly man named Harvey for his lemon meringue pie. Next came the second-place award, which went to Sandie Ballard for her southern caramel pecan pie. Now, for the moment of truth. The emcee cleared his throat, then reached for the trophy, which he held aloft in his left hand, while speaking into the microphone in his right. "We've got our pie category winner, folks! Winnie Washington of Wayfarers Inn takes the prize for her coconut cream meringue pie!"

A rousing cheer went up from the crowd. The emcee handed Winnie her trophy.

"Ms. Washington has taken both the pie and bread categories, which makes her our top baker. She will represent Washington County at the state competition in Columbus later this month. If she takes the prize there, she will win a lifetime supply of Rising Star products and a cruise ship vacation with a celebrity master chef." He thrust the microphone into Winnie's face. "Do you have anything you'd like to say?"

"I...I...I..." Winnie shook her head. "I'm just so honored. And so stunned."

Another cheer went up from the crowd. Janice watched as Winnie took her spot center stage. As soon as the pictures were taken, she and Georgia headed right for the Inn Crowd, who offered exuberant congratulations. "Thanks. I just can't believe it." Winnie shook her head. "I thought I was a goner at the half-way point. I looked in the oven, and the meringue on my pie was lopsided. I had to give it a nudge to level it off, but it worked just fine." She turned to Georgia and gave her a tight hug. "And knowing you were there ready to get anything I needed took a load off my mind. Thank you."

"I'm just so honored you chose me as your helper. You're so welcome." The young woman looked elated. "I can't remember when I've ever had so much fun. Though I thought I might faint from the heat at one point. I still can't believe they held a contest like this outdoors in August."

"Well, speaking of fun, they're about to give away samples of all of the goods. I say we head to the cake booth and fill up on our favorites." Robin took off through the crowd, and Winnie returned to the stage to offer sample bites of her pie to audience members.

"Well, I guess we've lost Robin for the day." Tess laughed. "I'd rather start with pie samples, myself."

Janice agreed. "Yes, let's make the rounds and sample the wares, shall we?"

They walked together to the stage, where the bakers offered tantalizing bites of the pies they had just baked. Janice took a couple of nibbles of lemon meringue, which tasted delicious. Before long, the three friends ended up in front of the unfamiliar blonde.

The woman extended her hand and smiled. "Hello, ladies. I'm Sandie Ballard." When Sandie released her hold on Janice's hand, she reached for a business card at the end of her table and handed one to LuAnn. "I just opened my shop, the Better Batter, this past week."

"And you're already giving our Winnie a run for her money in the pie category." Janice took a taste of the yummy sample. "For goodness' sake, you've got chocolate and caramel mixed in with these pecans."

"I call it my turtle pecan pie." Sandie beamed. "You can buy the pecan turtle at my new bakery. It's my Tuesday special." She pointed to the stack of pink and lime-green business cards. "Take as many of those as you like and hand them out. The more, the merrier."

Janice took one and pressed it into her purse.

Tess licked her lips. "It's mind-boggling how many different types of pies and cakes there are in the world."

Janice cleared her throat in an attempt to send a quiet message to Tess—*"Stop fraternizing with the enemy."* Not that Sandie Ballard was really an enemy, but there was no point in sending the café's customers to a new shop, after all.

"Hey, let's head over to the cake booth." Tess nudged Janice with her elbow. "I want to get a taste of Winnie's cookie-butter cake." She took off toward the cake table with Janice on her heels.

The women made their way to the cake samples, and before long everyone was nibbling.

"This cookie-butter cake is the finest thing I've ever put in my mouth," Tess declared. "I can't believe Winnie didn't win!" When she finished her sample, she clasped her hands together and grinned. "Say, all of these baked goods have given me an idea. What if we put together a little marketing campaign to help the inn capitalize on Winnie's win?"

"What sort of marketing campaign?" Janice asked as she took another bite of cake.

"Oh, I don't know. Did you see the big banner advertising today's event? Maybe we hang something like that over the front door of the inn to share the news of Winnie's win."

Janice shrugged. "Okay. That doesn't sound too extreme."

LuAnn's eyes flashed with sudden excitement. "What if we offered a 20 percent discount and a free loaf of bread to the first dozen people to book a room at the inn?"

Tess looked a bit perplexed by this notion. Janice felt a little confused herself.

"Local people, you mean?" she asked. "Or will out-of-towners get the loaves of bread when they arrive for their stay? If so, Winnie might be giving away bread for months to come."

LuAnn shook her head. "Well, I don't think the locals themselves will stay at the inn. But if they get friends or relatives to book a room, they could get a loaf of Winnie's bread as a commission. We'd say that the rooms have to be booked between now and Wednesday. That way the baking won't drag on forever. They book a room, they get a loaf of bread. It's that simple."

"Sounds like a lot of work for Winnie."

"I don't mind, Janice."

Janice jumped when she heard Winnie's voice behind her. "Are you done giving out samples?"

"Coconut cream pie doesn't last very long," Winnie replied. She turned to LuAnn. "Really, I bake so frequently anyway. Sounds like a fun way to entice people to try out the inn."

"I would agree to that," said Tess, "if we limit the eligible nights to Monday through Thursday, no holidays, and to this calendar year."

"Perfect." LuAnn looked around. "I'll see if I can track down that reporter. Maybe he'll add this information to his article. It should be in Monday's paper."

Winnie pointed. "Speaking of the reporter, I see he's still talking to Sandie Ballard." She reached for a sample of cake.

Janice looked in the direction she'd pointed. "Right. Looks like he's got her posing for a photo with her red ribbon. Oh, look! She's holding a piece of her cake for the picture. Fun."

Winnie stopped eating her cake and gave the man another look. "He tried to get my picture earlier when he was backstage before the event."

"He was backstage?" This took Janice by surprise.

Winnie shrugged. "Well, you know. For the article. Going from baker to baker, asking about their ingredients, and so on."

Janice pondered Winnie's words. "That seems a bit intrusive."

"It felt like it to me, but the other contestants didn't seem to mind. At first some of them seemed a little put off by him— until he explained that he was a reporter. Then a couple of them started talking about themselves like they were superstars. That's when he approached me and asked to take my picture."

"Did you let him?" Tess asked.

"Yes, but I had sweat pouring down my face, thanks to the heat. I'm sure I looked just lovely. Nothing like that beauty queen over there." She gestured to Sandie.

Janice patted her on the arm. "Beautiful or not, she couldn't beat our Winnie."

"But she still got second place, and she made the best cake, so that should tell you something," Winnie countered. "Apparently she's really good."

"But nobody, and I mean nobody, can beat our very own Winnie Washington from Wayfarers Inn." Tess spread her arms wide, as if showing off a banner. "Marietta's own Rising Star! I can see it now. Maybe we'll even use the Rising Star colors, just to make a point. How does that sound, Winnie? Can we start spreading the word about the free loaves of bread?"

"Sure. I'll need some help in the kitchen, but I can probably get them baked on Monday, ready for pickup on Tuesday and Wednesday."

"Perfect! I'll let Hank know right away." Tess took off toward the reporter, a woman on a mission.

Janice could tell Winnie was enjoying the flattering comments. And why not? She certainly deserved all the accolades this day could bring.

CHAPTER TWO

O n the Monday following the competition, reservations came rolling in, one after the other. Winnie and Georgia worked with fervor after the café lunch crowd left, kneading loaf after loaf of bread dough.

The Inn Crowd took turns visiting with their newest guest at the inn, a Mrs. Reena Newberry, from Pennsylvania. The elderly woman had arrived in style early that afternoon, dropped off by a limousine driver. She emerged from the vehicle in a bright teal ensemble with exaggerated floral print. Her jewelry and hair clip matched perfectly, as did her teal sandals. If you looked closely enough you could see every bluish vein in the backs of her hands, every lumpy joint. She wore her thin white hair in an upsweep, but tendrils had loosened from their pins and framed her face. Janice found her charming. She led the way to Sunshine and Daisies on the third floor, where Reena explained that she needed to take a nap until suppertime.

Janice headed back to the kitchen to offer her help to Winnie and Georgia, who were up to their elbows in yeasty bread dough. Winnie measured each risen blob of dough with great care, then dropped it into a loaf pan to rise again.

They were interrupted midafternoon by the reporter, Hank Clive, who showed up with an oversized bag of camera equipment, insisting he needed more photos for an upcoming feature story he wanted to do on Winnie. He pulled out his camera and started to take pictures of the café, then turned to Janice.

"I wanted to ask more detailed questions about Winnie's history as a baker. And I thought I'd snag a few more photos of the inn to tie into the story." He scribbled something down in his notebook. "I'm guessing Winnie's pretty busy again today. This is the day she was going to bake the loaves for your marketing strategy, right?"

"Yes, the first few loaves just went into the oven," Janice said.

"My editor is really excited about this article," he added. "He wants to know where she came from, how she learned to bake, any special tips she might want to give other bakers, that sort of thing. I was hoping to snag a couple of pictures of her at work in the kitchen."

"Well, I can ask her, but today probably isn't the best day for that. Winnie is really busy making the bread."

Hank frowned. "Hmm. That's a shame." Then his face cleared. "Well, I hope I can talk her into it. People always love pictures. Draws them into the story. I was thinking of doing a big splash piece. It'll be great for business. I think it would capture a lot of attention."

"I'll go find out." Janice left the room and returned less than a minute later with Winnie, who looked irritated at having been bothered. Georgia followed on her heels, looking nervous.

"I've got bread in the oven," Winnie grumbled.

"Yes, I'll do my best to make this quick." He snapped a photo of her, and Winnie flinched.

"I was already in the paper this morning," she protested. "That's enough publicity to last me a lifetime."

"That was a piece about the competition," he countered. "What I'm talking about is a feature article, based completely on you, Winnie. I want to see you shine like the star you are."

She reluctantly agreed but fussed at the interruption it posed to her baking. Janice didn't blame her. This day was hard enough for Winnie without having Hank Clive under-foot. With twelve loaves of bread to bake and the usual guests to serve, tensions were running high in the kitchen.

Much to Winnie's relief, Hank finally asked his last ques-tion and took his last picture. After he left, Tess and LuAnn headed to the office to sort through the reservations. Janice took care of tidying up the café, then found Winnie alone in the kitchen.

"Where's Georgia?" Janice asked, looking around.

"I sent her out several minutes ago to dump some trash. I have no idea what's taking her so long."

Janice walked through the mudroom to the back door. When she opened it, she was stunned to see Georgia talking with Sandie Ballard. They were standing far enough away from the building that she couldn't hear what they were saying, and they didn't notice her in the doorway. But she could tell from their postures and gestures that it was an intense conver-sation. When had Sandie arrived, and what did she want with

Georgia? And what was with the large bakery bag Sandie was carrying? Surely she wasn't trying to entice Georgia with her sweets. Was she?

Janice walked back into the kitchen, more perplexed than ever.

"Well, did you find her?"

"Hmm?" Janice looked Winnie's way. "Oh, yes. She's still out back, talking to…" Better not stir up Winnie any more than she already was. "One of the neighbors."

"Well, tell her to get back in here. We've got a lot of baking left to do."

When Georgia arrived inside she seemed very nervous. The usually talkative young woman suddenly had nothing to say. She did everything she could to avoid Janice's gaze.

By eight o'clock that evening, twelve loaves of bread sat on the kitchen counter, each sealed in a large storage bag. Winnie was busy at the stove frying sausage for the breakfast casserole she would serve their guests in the morning, while Georgia chopped onions and green peppers.

Janice finished drying the last loaf pan and put it in the cupboard. "Is there anything I can do to help you all get ready for the morning?"

Winnie looked up from the sausage. "No, Georgia and I can handle the rest. It shouldn't take too much longer." She waved her spatula at Janice. "You've been a great help with the bread. We'll finish up here and get on home."

Janice rolled her shoulders and neck. "That sounds good. Why don't you all come in a little late in the morning? The three of us can get the breads out of the freezer and put the casseroles in the oven."

Winnie stopped stirring the sausage and looked at Georgia, whose eyes would rival Huck's when he wanted a bite from the table. She chuckled. "I think Georgia would short-sheet my bed if I said no to that."

Georgia went to Winnie and gave her a hug. "I don't even know what that is," she said, grinning. "But I'm willing to learn if it means I can sleep past five."

Janice laughed. "It's a deal then. See you all in the morning."

Sometime around nine o'clock the Inn Crowd headed upstairs to their private quarters on the fourth floor. They parted ways in the hallway where Janice reached down to give their dog Huck a scratch behind the ears. An hour later she fell into bed and was asleep within minutes. Sometime during the night she woke to hear Huck in the hallway, scratching at the stairway door and whining. By the time she got up and got her robe and slippers on to take him out, he'd quit and was content on the couch, so she went back to bed.

Janice could hardly believe it when her alarm went off early Tuesday morning. It felt as if she'd only slept minutes, not hours. She did her best not to groan aloud as she rolled out of bed and prepared for her day.

She entered the kitchen and saw the dozen loaves of bread Winnie had left on the table. The kitchen still held the lingering smells of bread, sausage, and onion, and it wasn't long until Janice added a coffee aroma to the mix.

Tess and LuAnn trailed into the kitchen soon after Janice. Janice handed mugs of coffee all around and then started getting the muffins and scones out of the freezer. "I forgot to tell you all that yesterday I saw Georgia behind the inn talking to Sandie. It seemed like they were arguing about something."

Tess turned on the oven and pulled the casseroles out of the refrigerator. "What could they have to argue about? I didn't even know they knew each other."

"I didn't either," Janice said. "Apparently, they do."

LuAnn got busy wrapping silverware in napkins. "I don't know," she said. "It probably wasn't anything more nefarious than arguing which was best, Winnie's cookie-butter cake or Sandie's black forest cake."

"It seemed more intense than that," Janice insisted.

"Well, if it's important, we'll know it soon enough," said Tess.

Silence reigned for a while as they worked to get breakfast ready. They heard the bell over the front door jingle, and then in a minute Robin entered the kitchen. "How are you ladies this morning?" Ever cheerful and skilled in all things helpful, Robin was a valuable employee. She could unstop a drain, soothe a rankled guest, and clean a room faster than most people could unwind the vacuum cord.

After exchanging greetings, Robin got herself a mug of coffee and went out to the café to prep for the guests' breakfast at seven and for the customers who would start arriving by eight.

Janice was just testing the casseroles' temperatures when Winnie and Georgia came in the back door. Winnie had a frown on her face.

"That's funny," she said. "I guess I was so stressed last night when I left that I forgot to lock the kitchen door behind me." She put her bag down. "Or has one of you already been outside?"

"We haven't touched that door," said LuAnn.

Janice shut the oven door. "I'm not surprised, though, Winnie," she said. "And don't beat yourself up about it. You were exhausted last night. No one could blame you for forgetting something like that."

"Of course not," said Tess. "And no harm was done. Everything is just as it should be in here."

"Well, that's a relief," said Winnie.

Georgia went to the sink to wash her hands. "How did we come out with the reservations?" she asked. "Did the discount and the bread incentive work?"

All eyes went to Tess, the bookkeeping guru of the Inn Crowd. She smiled. "It sure did," she said. "We had nine people call yesterday and make reservations. That means three more deals are left."

"I imagine people will be coming around today to get their bread," said Janice. "So, Tess, if you'd leave a list of who the loaves should go to at the front desk, that'd work, I think."

"I can do that," said Tess, nodding.

Winnie groaned. "If we could go an entire day without mentioning bread, please, I'd be very grateful." She grabbed her apron off the peg. "Now let's get this show on the road."

After the café's breakfast run, Winnie decided a trip to the grocery store was in order, so she left Georgia in charge of the chicken soup, just coming to a simmer on the stove.

Janice, Tess, and LuAnn turned their attention to the new banner, which had just arrived. They stepped outside to have a look. Janice couldn't help but gasp.

"Wow, that's something!" Okay, maybe the colors were a little too bright, and yes, it was big, but that was the point, after all. She smiled as she read the words: *Welcome to Wayfarers Inn, Home of Marietta's own Rising Star, Winnie Washington.*

"Don't you think it's a little...large?" LuAnn narrowed her eyes to slits, as if willing the lettering to shrink.

Georgia joined them outside. "I like it." She twisted one of her curls with her index finger. "Maybe one day my name will be on a banner like that. If I hang out with Winnie long enough, I mean. I still have a lot to learn between now and then."

Janice patted her on the arm. "From everything I've observed, you're doing great, Georgia. Your parents were right. You were born to cook. And we're so happy to have you here."

"Thank you." The young woman's deep brown eyes shimmered with delight. "I just feel so thankful that Winnie took me under her wing. She's the best. And I had a blast at that competition. Highlight of my life so far."

Janice looked her in the eye. "So what was up with you and Sandie yesterday?"

Georgia jumped to attention. "Oh my goodness, I'm supposed to be keeping an eye on everything in the kitchen until Winnie gets back from the grocery store. She's going to kill me if that chicken soup gets scorched!" She bounded toward the front door and disappeared inside.

All right then, Janice thought. *So much for not being nefarious.*

Several of the locals joined them at the front of the inn, and before long they had quite a crowd staring up at the new sign. Many were still buzzing about the feature story that had come out in today's paper. Others were there to eat lunch at the café. Janice saw a few in the crowd who had taken advantage of their discount offer. Tess and LuAnn made a trip to the kitchen to get their bread for them and handed the loaves out.

From the midst of the crowd a woman waved her hand to get Janice's attention. Janice recognized her as Brandy Sue, the petite forty-something who worked as a receptionist at Much Kneaded Massage.

"Is there still time to make a reservation and get the discount and a free loaf of bread?" Brandy Sue asked. "Or am I too late?"

"Yes, we've got three spots left," Janice assured her. "I'll give the bread to you as soon as you book your room."

"Great!" said Brandy Sue. "Let me just make a phone call, and I'll meet you inside."

Brad Grimes, their Realtor friend, arrived moments later, loaded down with grocery bags.

"Have you done our shopping for us, Brad?" Janice asked.

"No." He gestured with his head to Winnie, who came barreling up the sidewalk with the rest of the groceries. The crowd began to cheer the moment they saw her. For a moment, she looked as if she might turn and run the opposite direction, but she held steady.

"Let me help with that, Winnie." Janice extended her arms and reached for a couple of the grocery bags.

Winnie shook her head. "No, thanks. If you take one, all of 'em will topple. I have a system. And besides, Brad took the heavier ones. But I would be grateful if someone would open the door for me."

"Why are you coming in the front, anyway?" Tess took a step toward the front door. "Why not go through the kitchen, as usual?"

"I saw all of the activity over here, and my curiosity kicked in." Winnie glanced up at the sign, and her mouth fell open. "Well, that would be hard to miss."

"Don't you like it?" LuAnn asked.

Winnie grunted. "I think we've already established that I don't do well with lots of attention. You saw me yesterday when the reporter was here. I was a nervous wreck. I almost dropped a bag of sugar in front of him. That would have made a great picture."

"Oh, Hank Clive interviewed you?" Brad shifted the bags in his arms. "Glad to see he's meeting people. He's new to town."

"He nearly wore me out, asking so many questions at the competition. I could hardly stay focused on my pie. But can we talk about this after we get inside?"

21

Janice nodded. "Of course." She pulled the oversized front door open and gestured for Winnie to enter. Brad followed behind them. LuAnn took charge of getting the guests seated in the café while Janice and Tess followed Winnie and Brad to the kitchen, where they found Georgia hard at work stirring the chicken soup and preparing Parker House rolls. The kitchen smelled like a combination of freshly baked bread, cinnamony cookies, and chicken soup.

Winnie plopped groceries down on the countertop and sighed, as if relieved from unloading the weight of it all. "It's been a fruitful morning, to say the least."

Brad set his bags down and stretched his arms. "Well, you ladies have been praying for more guests, and I'd say this marketing strategy got you what you prayed for."

"Speaking of more guests, I need to take a loaf out to Brandy Sue," Janice said. "She's making a reservation."

"That makes ten!" Tess clasped her hands together. "Great job, team. Only two more!"

"So glad I got all of that bread baked yesterday," Winnie said. "Not sure how I would have managed otherwise."

Janice grabbed a loaf of bread and carried it out to the lobby, where she found Brandy Sue chatting on her phone. Minutes later, the reservation was made, and Janice was heading back to the kitchen, where Robin and Taylor, their right-hand employees, were hefting trays of soup to carry into the café.

Winnie worked alongside Georgia dishing up bowls of soup. She glanced up with a smile. "I struggled to get through the checkout line at the grocery store. Everybody and their brother stopped me to chat. At first I was worried about holding up the line, but after a while I stopped fretting because no one seemed to care."

"You're a local hero, Winnie." Brad gave her an admiring smile.

"They all wanted to hear about the competition—how I felt, what ingredients I used, where the recipes came from, what I plan to bake in the state finals, if I had any baking secrets or tips, and so on." She paused, and a concerned look came over her face. "At least they weren't as nosy as that reporter. He almost drove me mad asking question after question yesterday when he was here."

"Well, that's what an interview is, Winnie," Janice explained. "Reporters are always thorough."

"Right, but he distracted me. And he kept trying to come into my kitchen. I put an end to that notion right away. No one steps in here unless they work here." She smiled at Brad. "Or unless they're special friends, of course."

Brad smiled back at her. "Hank is new on the job," he explained. "I'm sure he's just excited."

"Maybe so." Winnie plopped down in a chair at the table and started fanning herself.

Janice took the empty grocery bags and folded them neatly, then tucked them into a lower cabinet.

Brad moved toward the kitchen door. "If you will excuse me, I think I'll join the others in the café. Can't wait to taste some of that chicken soup." He grinned at them and left the room.

Janice paused and gazed at her friend, noticing the exhaustion on Winnie's face, the wrinkle lines on her forehead. "Have you forgiven us yet?" she asked after a moment. "For all of this extra work, I mean."

Winnie wiped a loose hair off her face with the back of her hand. Her shoulders slumped forward, and she released a sigh. "I love you, and I love the inn, Janice. You know that. There's nothing to forgive."

Janice felt a sense of relief but still wasn't convinced Winnie was okay. "I know you love us, and we adore you too. But this marketing idea of ours has increased your workload exponentially, and I'm sorry about that."

"I'm here to help." Georgia stopped working and looked up with a broad grin. "And I'm a hard worker."

"She is, at that," Winnie said. "So no apologies necessary."

Janice couldn't help but agree that Georgia was a hard worker. But her suspicious behavior yesterday left a few question marks in Janice's mind.

Before she could give it much thought, LuAnn buzzed into the kitchen. "Okay, everyone's settled. Well, mostly, anyway. Taylor and Robin can take it from here. I wanted to let you ladies know that I stopped by the historical society yesterday. Margaret is talking about creating a new kitchen display from the 1800s, capitalizing on the baking aspect. You've inspired everyone, Winnie. You should be very proud of yourself. I know we are."

"There's a buzz in the air, for sure." Winnie winced as she shifted her position. "But hopefully the excitement will wear off soon. I'm the same Winnie Washington who cooks for Wayfarers Inn, as always. Only...busier. Soon I'll have more guests to cook for."

LuAnn raised her finger. "Speaking of more guests, I put together a little list of repairs in a couple of the rooms. Nothing big, but I've called in Thorn. He'll be coming by later today to assess the situation, then he'll come back later in the week to do the work. Sound okay?"

"Perfect," Janice agreed. Their handyman would make sure everything was in tip-top condition.

LuAnn headed out of the kitchen toward the office. Janice and Tess followed along behind her.

Before they made it to the check-in desk, the front door burst open, and a woman rushed inside. Janice recognized Sally, the local dog groomer, at once. She carried a mangled loaf of bread, which she shoved in Janice's direction.

"Would you care to explain this?"

"I...I...well, that's a freshly baked loaf of bread, Sally," Janice responded. "I gave it to you about thirty minutes ago, but it didn't look like that."

"My dachshund, Copper, got a hold of it, and that's how I found out what Winnie had done."

"What Winnie had done?" None of this made sense.

"What's this about, Sally?" Tess asked.

"I'll tell you what it's about." Sally's volume rose a few decibels. "But first you get her out here so I can talk to her myself."

LuAnn rushed to the kitchen and returned a moment later with a very frazzled Winnie.

"What's happening?" Winnie asked. "Is the building on fire?"

"I want to know why you did it, Winnie." Sally pressed the mangled loaf into Winnie's hands.

"Why I did what?"

"Why you put something in that bread that could have potentially harmed me or my sweet Copper. Are you trying to kill us, or is this some type of clever marketing scheme?"

For a moment, Winnie said nothing. Janice watched in amazement as her friend's eyes flooded with tears. She half expected her to run from the room in confusion or embarrassment. Instead, Winnie did something completely unexpected.

She fainted.

CHAPTER THREE

"Goodness gracious goat!" Janice couldn't help herself. The moment she saw her friend land on the floor, the familiar expression shot out. "Someone call 911."

"I—I didn't mean to hurt her." Sally paled and looked as if she might go down as well. "I was just upset. You know how it is when you're upset. You say things without thinking. I didn't mean to hurt her."

Upset over what, Janice still wasn't sure. The accusation was confusing, if not ridiculous. But that would have to wait. Right now they needed to take care of Winnie. Janice knelt on the floor, and Tess joined her, checking the inside of Winnie's wrist.

"Her pulse is strong, and she's breathing fine," Tess said. "I'm sure she just passed out. She's been slaving in that hot kitchen all morning, then she went to the grocery store in this heat, and now this."

"Oh dear. And all over a stupid loaf of bread. Now I'm sorry I ever complained in the first place." Sally knelt down across from them. "Winnie, wake up!"

She waved her hands over Winnie's face, as if trying to rouse her. Unfortunately, Winnie didn't budge. Janice watched the rise and fall of her chest, concerned about her friend's breathing. Fortunately, it remained steady and strong. But Winnie remained unconscious.

Seconds later, Brad joined them. "I heard the commotion from the café." He took one look at Winnie, and his eyes widened. "Do you need me to call 911?" He reached for his phone and also knelt beside Winnie on the floor.

"I used to faint periodically. Low blood pressure." Reena Newberry's quavering voice sounded from beside them. "No need to panic. The answer is smelling salts. She will come to, I assure you."

"Smelling salts? We don't have anything like that." LuAnn pulled her cell phone out of her pocket. "I'm calling 911."

"I seem to recall that a lemon does the trick as well," Reena said. "A friend used it on me once when I'd left my smelling salts at home."

"Now that, we do have." Tess sprinted out of the room and reappeared a couple of minutes later with lemon wedges in a small bowl. She passed off a wedge of lemon to Brad, who held it under Winnie's nose. At first, nothing happened. Then, after a few seconds, Winnie began to stir. She looked rather discombobulated as she batted at the lemon. "Wh-what in the world?" She tried to sit but ended up with her head on the floor once more. "H-how did I get down here?"

"Just rest easy, Winnie." Brad held the lemon under her nose again. "No sudden moves."

"I...I'm trying, but I don't understand why you're making lemonade at a time like this. There's too much work to be done."

"I'm not." Brad pulled the lemon away.

"He's saving your life," Reena called out.

"Saving my life?" Winnie tried once again to sit up and finally managed to do it with Brad's help. "Am I dying?" She rubbed the back of her head.

"You fainted," Sally explained. "And I'm afraid it's my fault. I came to complain about the loaf of bread you gave me. It had laminated paper inside of it. Copper almost ate it. Could have hurt him. That lamination is sharp on the edges, you know."

"What?" Winnie pinched her eyes shut and then opened them again. "I did what?"

"Could you tell us more about what you found, Sally?" Brad asked.

"Well, I..." The woman looked back and forth between Brad and Winnie, who still looked out of sorts. "It was right in the middle of the loaf and could have killed my dog."

Winnie gasped and attempted to stand but didn't make it. She settled back down on the floor. "This has to be a mistake. I didn't put any such thing in those loaves of bread. You're playing some kind of trick on us."

"I'm not, I assure you." Sally looked irritated at this accusation. "What would be the point of that?"

Brad put his hands up. "Sally, do you have this paper with you?"

Sally looked at him, her eyes shooting daggers. "I do. I'll show it to you, and then you'll know how dangerous it could have been for my Copper." She began rummaging around in the large bag that was slung over her shoulder.

Winnie sat up and cupped her head in her hands, still looking faint. "I just don't know how anything could have gotten in my bread."

"I suppose anything is possible," Georgia said with a feeble shrug. "We were working so hard and fast yesterday."

"That's putting it mildly," Reena said. "This place was a madhouse, yesterday and today. Not really sure what I've gotten myself into, but here I am."

Yes, here she was. Right in the thick of things, Janice observed.

"Do you think you might've dropped one of the flour labels into the dough, Winnie?" Brad asked.

"Of course not." Winnie tried to stand but was still too woozy.

"Here it is!" Sally crowed. She held up something pink. "Proof positive."

"This is no label." Janice took the slip. "This is a note, written on pink stationery and then laminated."

"Pink stationery?" Tess and LuAnn spoke in unison.

"I would almost understand if you were trying to put some sort of fun message inside the bread," Sally said. "But this one was so...menacing."

"Oh, man." Winnie leaned forward as if feeling faint again.

Sally pointed at the note. "It seems to me you're shooting yourselves in the foot. If this is the way you ladies market your inn, then I shouldn't imagine you'll get many new guests."

"This is a marketing ploy?" Reena asked. "Isn't it enough that you had to hang that ridiculous banner out front? Now you're sending messages in bread?"

"No." Winnie shook her head. "I didn't put any messages in the bread—positive or negative. This whole thing is crazy." She put her hands on her head, as if to stabilize herself or clear her thoughts.

Brad reached for the slip of laminated paper. Janice handed it to him and then watched as he examined it.

"What does it say?" Tess walked over to Brad and glanced down at the paper. Her breath caught in her throat as she read the words, "Stay away from Wayfarers Inn—or else."

"Now, I know that's not Winnie's handwriting," Janice said. "I've seen her grocery lists hundreds of times, and her hand is much neater."

"Thank you. I pride myself on my handwriting." Winnie shook her head. "And I can assure you, I never wrote any such thing or baked any slips of paper into my bread. And we don't even have a laminating machine, do we?"

"Actually, we do," Tess said. "In the office. I'm pretty sure the last time I saw it, it was caked in dust." She was quick to turn to Reena and add, "Not that we're dusty around here, mind you. It just hasn't been used in ages, is all."

Sally rose and began to pace the room. "Well, someone did this, and they were trying to send a clear message. Trust me when I say it did the trick. Startled me, for sure."

All eyes shifted to Georgia. She put her hands up, as if under arrest. "Don't look at me. Just because I'm helping in the kitchen doesn't mean I'm up to mischief. Besides, I love Wayfarers Inn. Why would I do anything to hurt you ladies?"

Janice pondered the young woman's words. She hoped Georgia could be trusted, but it never hurt to keep a watchful eye out, especially in light of her meeting with Sandie Ballard out back yesterday. The Inn Crowd had been bamboozled by a kitchen helper once before, after all. Janice shivered as she thought about how Kylie had tried to get revenge on LuAnn with some poisonous mushrooms.

"This has to be a fluke." Tess shook her head.

"It can't be a fluke," LuAnn countered. "This was deliberate."

Tess nodded. "I guess you're right."

"I vote for calling the police." Reena turned and walked toward the elevator. "But then again, I probably don't get a vote."

"No, please. Not yet." Winnie extended her hand. "Let me see that note. Maybe I can make sense of it."

They passed it her way, and she looked it over, eyes wide. Then she shook her head. "I'm bumfuzzled, ladies. No idea where that came from or what it means."

"I agree that we should involve the police." Tess pulled out her phone. "They can help us sort it out."

"I just hate all of this attention." Winnie looked light-headed once again.

"I can't fathom how they knew the slips of paper wouldn't burn up," LuAnn said.

"Maybe they thought the lamination would serve as some sort of protection," Brad said. "That would be my guess."

"It almost worked." Janice held up the slip of paper and examined it closely. "It's remarkable how the print is still so detailed. I would have thought the moisture from the dough would have caused it to smear or something."

Winnie nodded. "Whoever did this is either a baker, or they experimented until they made it work."

"I agree that we can probably figure this out if we just focus," Brad said. "So let's talk this through. You started baking when, Winnie?"

"Yesterday afternoon. Georgia and I made the dough and set it to rise, then put it in the loaf pans and let it rise again. We had to work in batches because I don't have twelve loaf pans. But we got it all done by around seven or so and then bagged them once they'd cooled."

"Did you notice any suspicious activity while you were baking?" Brad asked.

"Other than that reporter trying to weasel his way into my kitchen, no. But you can be sure my eyes will be wide open from now on."

Janice heard a very faint voice calling, "What's your emergency?" She looked at Tess standing beside her. Tess looked at her, startled. "Oh, goodness! I must've accidentally called 911." She clamped a hand over her mouth, then pulled it away and stared at her phone, still in her hand.

A woman's voice came through from the other end of the line. "911. What is your emergency?"

Tess continued to stare at the phone as if it were a snake. "What do I do?" She put it on speakerphone just in time for everyone to hear the dispatcher ask, "Is anyone there? What is your emergency?"

"I, well, a friend fainted," Tess managed.

"Do you need an ambulance, ma'am?"

"No!" Winnie cried out. "If they send an ambulance over here, I'll never forgive any of you. Just let me get back to work."

"No. I think she's going to be okay," Tess responded.

The woman kept talking. "As a precaution, I need you to position the patient on her back and raise her legs above her heart level. About twelve inches or so should do."

"For pity's sake." Winnie shook her head. "That's ridiculous." She tried once more to stand but still looked a little wobbly. Janice gestured for her to sit back down. Brad patted her on the shoulder.

The dispatcher continued with her instructions. "If there's a need to loosen anything—a belt, or collar or any constrictive clothing—please do that as well."

Winnie put her hand up in the air, and her eyes bugged. "If *anyone* touches my clothing, I'm going to come up swinging."

The dispatcher stayed on the line long enough to make sure Winnie was truly going to be all right, then she ended the call. Janice's gaze returned to Winnie, who insisted on getting up off the floor. With Tess's and Georgia's help, she was soon seated in a nearby chair.

"Now, let's start again." Winnie extended her hand in Sally's direction. "If you don't mind, please give me that loaf of bread so I can give it a closer look."

Sally passed the mangled loaf her way. "I got home and set it on the table. Copper must've hopped up on the chair, then the tabletop. Next thing you know, he's on the table, digging in.

I happened to glance his way just as that piece of laminated paper went straight into his mouth. I'm so glad he didn't choke."

"I don't know how this happened," Winnie said. "But I know how to fix it, at least for now. I'll stay late today and make another loaf for you, Sally."

Janice couldn't believe Winnie would even offer, after the crazy couple of days she'd had. And how could she bake in this condition?

"That's not necessary, Winnie." Sally sighed. "I feel awful, now that I know you didn't do this on purpose."

"If you change your mind, let me know. I can always bake an extra loaf tomorrow or the next day."

Janice took the loaf of bread and examined it closely, then gave the slip of laminated paper another once-over. "Very strange," she said. Who could have done such a thing...and why?

CHAPTER FOUR

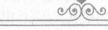

August 4, 1860

Prudence kneaded the large mound of bread dough and gave it a firm smack with her fist. It was midafternoon, and the late summer heat was causing beads of sweat to trickle down her back. She felt sticky and uncomfortable.

Regardless, she had to forge ahead. She ignored the discomfort and kept working. Content with her progress, she covered the ball of dough with a clean cloth and set it aside to rise. In this heat, it shouldn't take as long as usual for the dough to prove.

Prudence turned her attentions to tidying up the inn's large kitchen. Dishes were piled high in the sink, a sure sign of the busy day she'd had. A slight creak of the floorboards startled her, and she turned, expecting to find someone standing there. Instead, she found the room empty. Odd. Probably just the wind. She placed her hand on her heart and willed it to slow down. These days, one never knew who might appear.

As she reached for the broom, a shadow in the corner of the room appeared to move. "Mercy!" Prudence let out a cry as her gaze landed on a white man—a very young man—in a tattered shirt, holding his arm, which was covered in mud and blood. The man had pressed himself into the farthest spot in the kitchen, as if willing himself to disappear altogether.

"Thee nearly frightened me to death." Prudence took a couple of steps toward the man, who looked terrified. With wide brown eyes, he gazed at her, then blinked. He took a step forward, stumbled, and fell to the floor in a heap.

Prudence hurried to his side and knelt, examining him for other signs of injury. Nothing about the frightened man looked familiar to her. This was a stranger.

Beads of sweat dripped down the man's temples. His eyelids fluttered, and he groaned. His feet scrabbled on the floor, and he tried to get up.

"Wait," said Prudence, laying a hand on his uninjured arm. She went around to his back and put her hands under his shoulders. She lifted him as best she could and helped him settle into a kitchen chair.

She filled a glass with water from a pitcher and handed it to him. "Where has thee come from?" she asked. "What is thy name?"

The man drained the glass as if he hadn't had a drink in days. Priscilla refilled it for him, and he drained it again. Then he put the glass on the table. He bowed his head, and his lips moved, as if in prayer. When he looked up at her, his eyes were shining. "Praise God," he said. "He has blessed me this day and sent me straight to thee."

CHAPTER FIVE

On the morning after Winnie's fainting episode, Janice made her way through the busy café, helping Taylor and Robin out as they served the lunch guests. In spite of the fiasco with Sally's loaf of bread, the café was more crowded with customers than usual. It looked like the inn was on a winning streak, just like Winnie. Hopefully Sally wouldn't go to the paper with her story. Winnie had agreed to bake a new loaf of bread for her, after all.

Instead of fretting over the situation, Janice decided to stay focused on her remaining guests. She went from table to table serving coffee and offering more bread. The clinking of silverware against ceramic plates, coupled with the sound of nearly a dozen overlapping conversations, gave the café a welcoming feel, one that brought a great sense of contentment. And the fragrant aroma of coffee was the proverbial icing on the cake. Folks really seemed to be enjoying themselves, which made her heart happy.

Well, all but one.

Janice noticed Reena Newberry moving slowly toward the café. This morning's ensemble was a bright lime green, every item carefully matched, as always.

"Can I help you, Reena?" Janice asked.

"Am I too late for breakfast? After all of the chaos of the past two days I decided to sleep in."

"You're just in time for lunch," Janice said. "And I'm sorry you've been disturbed. We have had quite a few more people in and out than usual. And of course there was that bread fiasco."

"How is Winnie today?" Reena asked.

"Much better. She's back to her usual self."

"Good. I thought things were bad on the day I arrived, with that reporter hanging around. He was quite nosy. Asked me dozens of questions, even wanted to know if he could take photos of my room!"

Janice was stunned by this news. "My goodness, I hope you said no."

"Of course, but he put up a fight. He said it would help you ladies market the inn, but I didn't buy into that." She pursed her lips. "As if my being here had anything to do with this whole marketing scheme of yours." She paused, and crinkles formed around her eyes. "It doesn't, does it?"

"Of course not. I don't know what you mean."

"Don't you?"

Reena gave her a pensive look, one that Janice couldn't quite decipher. She also couldn't figure out why the woman would imply that her being here was in any way related to their plans for the inn.

Janice shook off her ponderings and led the way into the café. A couple of minutes later, Reena ordered a turkey sandwich. Janice went to the kitchen to fix it herself and then added a few potato chips on the side.

"Everything okay out there?" Georgia asked.

"Yes, just a lot busier than usual. But everyone seems happy." She lifted the plate with Reena's food and added, "Well, most everyone."

"No one's talking about my fainting episode yesterday, are they?" Winnie asked.

Janice shook her head. "No. I'm hoping that note was just a fluke or some sort of trick Sally's husband decided to play on her. Something like that."

She returned to the café and set the plate down in front of Reena. Reena's gaze tipped up in Janice's direction. With a shaky finger, the elderly woman pointed her way. "I'm a newcomer, and you might not take my advice, but I mean this to be helpful. You folks are so busy trying to make a name for yourselves that you've forgotten what's important here."

Whoa. It was quite an accusation, and one that caught Janice off guard.

Reena waved her hand toward the front door. "That banner out there, for one thing. I mentioned this yesterday, but it's worth saying again. It's tacky. I'm surprised the city let you get away with putting it up. It's not at all professional."

"I like the banner," Janice said.

Reena shook her head. "This is a historical building, one with a rich history, as you must know. You've tainted the look of it with that ridiculous thing. And another thing…you've kept Winnie so busy baking those silly loaves of bread that she's fallen down on the job with her meals. I waited eight minutes for my soup to arrive at lunch yesterday. And when I got it, it was cold."

"It was vichyssoise," Janice explained. "It's meant to be served cold. Perfect on a hot day, I might add. I had a bowl myself and thought it was delicious. I'm sorry you didn't prefer it."

"And another thing. Winnie's got that Georgie-person in her kitchen, doing much of the cooking while she bakes."

"I hope you can get to know Georgia a bit while you're here," Janice said. "She came all the way from Akron to be mentored by Winnie. When her family stayed with us earlier this summer they fell in love with Winnie's cooking and arranged the whole thing. Yes, she's doing a lot of the cooking and baking so Winnie can still keep up with the meals for the inn, but that was the plan when she arrived, to teach Georgia the ropes so she can one day own a restaurant of her own. She counts it a privilege to be with us, and we feel the same about her."

"Humph." Reena's nose wrinkled. She brushed her palms against her bright green slacks and leaned back in the chair.

Janice paused to think of something to say. Until now, Reena had been a delightful guest. Interesting, but delightful. LuAnn and Tess had taken a particular interest in her fashion choices. Now, if only the expression on her face matched the brightness of her clothing, wouldn't that be something?

"I feel like I'm staying in a cheap motel, not a lovely historical inn. It ruins the mood."

Ouch. The mood was being ruined, all right, but not by the banner. Pangs of embarrassment and frustration struck Janice, and she looked around to make sure none of the other guests had overheard. No one seemed to be paying attention. She mentally counted to ten before responding, in the hopes that she could keep her emotions under control. "I'm sorry you feel that way, Reena. Truly, I am. We will revisit the idea of keeping the banner, but I, for one, am happy to leave it up, since it promotes our dear Winnie, who's part of the Wayfarers Inn family."

LuAnn walked their way with a tea pitcher in hand. "Would you like some tea, Reena?"

"I suppose."

LuAnn filled a glass and set it in front of their guest. "I decided to help Robin and Taylor serve today. We've all had quite a workout. Today's crowd beats the last two days, hands down."

"Yes, I don't ever recall seeing it this crowded for lunch before," Janice agreed. "But that's a good thing, right?"

LuAnn gave the room another glance. "I suppose. Having customers is always a good thing, but I've got that same feeling I had as a kid when my rabbit had babies."

"Excuse me?" Reena looked up from her spot at the table. "Did you say something about rabbit? It's never been a favorite, and I can't imagine having it for lunch."

"Not on the menu, Reena." LuAnn chuckled. "When I was a kid, my rabbit had babies. And then the babies had babies. And before you knew it, our cage wasn't big enough to hold all the rabbits."

Janice drew the only logical conclusion she could come up with. "Let me get this straight. You're calling our café guests rabbits, and you want me to build a bigger cage?"

"It was just an illustration, silly." LuAnn laughed as she handed Reena a napkin. "But we are bursting at the seams. And yes, that's a good thing. But at some point, we have to realize that there are only so many rooms to book and only so many meals and sweets we can serve. I think it's realistic for us to pull back on the marketing a bit."

"Pull back on your marketing?" Reena put her hand to her ear, as if straining to hear. "Are you saying you're going to buy fewer groceries? How will you feed us?"

"Not that kind of marketing, Reena." LuAnn patted her on the shoulder, then turned her attention to Janice. "You know what I mean. Otherwise we'll wear ourselves ragged. I don't know about you, but I'm no good to anyone when I'm worn out."

"That's true," Reena put in. "And I suppose that's why you ladies haven't—" She shook her head. "Oh, never mind."

Janice couldn't help but wonder how Reena would have ended that sentence. Likely, with another speech about how tacky the sign out front was.

Reena grew quiet and then sipped her tea. "I have a bit of a headache, and I'm afraid it's put me in a mood. I apologize if I've come across as rude this morning."

"I'm sorry you're not feeling well." Janice patted Reena's hand. "Do you have something to take for the pain, or can I offer you something?"

"The caffeine in the tea should help." Reena looked around the busy café. "You were right about the rabbits, by the way."

"Oh?" Janice chuckled.

"This place is busier than ever. Guess that's why…" Reena shook her head. "Anyway, it's busy."

"Sure is. That's a good thing. We've been trying to build our business for a while now. Getting the word out is so important. That's how we end up with wonderful guests like you." Janice looked at Reena and smiled.

"Guests like me? Do you truly consider me a guest?"

"Well, of course, and we hope you have a lovely time with us, Reena."

"I have. So far." She took another sip of her tea and leaned back in her chair. "And I will stay as long as you feel necessary."

"As long as we feel necessary?"

"Well yes, of course. If you'll continue to have me."

"We love having you here, Reena. And we hope you're enjoying your room."

"Nothing like my home in Pittsburgh, but I've settled in nicely. I have no complaints."

Well, that was a novelty.

Janice left the café and headed to the kitchen, but was stopped by a woman she recognized as one of the town's librarians, Amy Wright. Janice would never have considered this petite woman intimidating, but she seemed pretty fired up today. Anger flamed in her eyes, and her voice sounded like a tea kettle about to boil over as she carried on about a loaf of bread she had received the morning prior, one with a not-so-friendly message inside.

"How dare Winnie send me a threat!" Mrs. Wright exclaimed. "That note was inflammatory, to say the least."

"What did it say?" Janice asked.

"Check into Wayfarers Inn, and you might just check out...permanently!"

CHAPTER SIX

Janice's breath caught in her throat. "Are you absolutely sure that's what it said, Mrs. Wright?"

"Of course I'm sure. Do you want to see the note yourself?"

"No, no, I trust you." She paused and tried to think of the right words to say to console the woman standing before her.

"I'm so sorry that happened to you, Mrs. Wright. I can assure you, Winnie did not write that note. Someone is attempting to sabotage her work and put the inn in a bad light. We're as shocked as you are, and terribly concerned. I do hope you believe me that we had nothing to do with this."

"I have no way of knowing someone else is to blame." The woman crossed her arms at her chest. "For all I know, you ladies are trying to send a message to the community."

"Why would we deliberately alienate our friends and neighbors?" Janice asked. "That doesn't make any sense. I promise, Winnie had nothing to do with those messages. None of us did. Please take my word on that and continue to visit us at the café. We so enjoy your visits."

"Humph." She shook her head. "I don't believe I'll be eating here until I'm sure it's safe. And you can go ahead and cancel my cousin's upcoming reservation while we're at it. I don't want her staying here now, not when I don't know who wrote that note. Maybe when all of this settles down. Until then—"

"I understand." Janice released a sigh. "But please don't give up on us altogether. I promise we're working on the problem. And it would appear we might need to call in the police, now that things are escalating."

"I would hope so." The woman huffed off in a snit, mumbling under her breath.

Janice walked into the kitchen, determined to calm her thoughts before saying anything to the others. She found Winnie seated in a chair, and Georgia and LuAnn fanning her with a couple of dishcloths.

"What's happening?" Janice rushed their way.

"Oh, I just got a little overheated," Winnie explained. "They're making a big fuss, but I'm fine."

"We tried to talk her into taking the rest of the morning off," LuAnn explained. "She wouldn't hear of it."

"It was just the heat from all the stovetop burners and oven going at once," Winnie argued. "I'm right as rain. And you all know that I've got a lot to do. I need to bake another loaf of bread for Sally. There's no time for lounging around."

Janice almost said, "Make that two loaves," but stopped short.

"We would feel better if you went home to rest for a couple of hours," LuAnn said.

"Yes, we certainly don't want to see you faint again." Janice rested her hand on her friend's arm, genuinely filled with concern. "We'll clean up in here, and please don't worry about baking any more bread. It's not necessary."

"Thank you." Winnie offered a weak smile. "But the truth is, I'm trying out a new pie recipe. I promised to have it done before I leave for the day. Brad is coming by to taste it, and I don't want to let him down."

"He mentioned that he was the lucky one," said LuAnn, smiling. "We're going out for dinner tonight, and he said he'd come by a little early to let Winnie know what he thinks of her pie."

"Yes, he's agreed to be my official taste tester."

LuAnn laughed. "I don't think you had to twist his arm very hard." She turned to the door. "I'm off to the office to catch up on some licensing paperwork."

Janice chuckled to herself. She would bet that Brad didn't have to have his arm twisted very hard to ask LuAnn to go to dinner with him either. No matter how much LuAnn protested that she and Brad were still just friends, Janice was pretty sure Brad didn't see it that way.

Tess entered the kitchen with an armload of dirty dishes. "It's a madhouse out there. But you'll be happy to know that I brought a smile to Reena Newberry's face by offering her one of your cookies, Winnie. I think the cinnamon did the trick. Not sure why she's so testy, anyway. I almost felt like I had disappointed her in some way."

"Strange you should say that," Janice said. "Because that's how she made me feel too."

"I can't figure her out." Tess walked over to the sink and began to fill it with water. She added detergent and then got to work washing dishes.

"I know how we can cheer her up," Georgia said. "Ask her to be your official cookie taste tester. She would probably love that, and it would make her feel included."

"Good idea." Winnie nodded. "I might just do that. But I still need to make this pie for Brad. I promised."

"Well, I guess I'll stop arguing and let you get back to baking," Janice said. "At least you've got Georgia to help you out. That's a relief." Janice smiled at Winnie's young protégé. "We're so happy you're enjoying your time here, honey. I think your parents would be proud of the progress you've made in the kitchen. And on weeks like this, I'm happy to have support for Winnie."

"Thanks." Georgia offered a shy smile as she tucked her hair behind her ears. "I'm always happy to help, and I'm learning so much. This has been an awesome experience so far."

"I'm so glad." Janice went over to dry dishes for Tess.

Winnie continued with her work as well, humming a familiar worship song as she made her pie. God bless Winnie and her music choices. One day it was hymns, the next, show tunes. Some folks just had a song in their hearts, and Winnie was definitely one of them.

"I'll tell you one thing you could do that would be a huge help, Janice." Winnie stopped humming and looked up from her mixing bowl. "If you're going out today, I've got a list of things I need from the grocery store. Would you mind passing it off to Marcus while you're out? I'll need them delivered by tomorrow morning."

"Actually, Tess is the one going out, but I'll make sure she gets the list."

"Great. Georgia wrote it all down on that notepad over there." She pointed to the countertop on the opposite side of the kitchen.

Janice walked over to retrieve the list but stopped short when she saw the pad it was written on.

Pink.

Lined paper.

Just like the laminated slips.

"Georgia?"

Georgia looked up from cleaning the stove. "Yes?"

Janice held up the notepad. "You made this list?"

"I sure did." Georgia set her rag down and took a few steps in Janice's direction. "Why? Did I forget something? I was sure I put down everything Winnie told me. I'm a little distracted, though, so it's possible."

"Oh, I don't know about that part. Just curious about this notepad you used. Where did you get it?"

"They were at the baking competition. See the header? It's got the Rising Star logo."

"Right. I see it." Still, she didn't remember seeing the notepads at the event. "Were they free?"

"Yep. I picked up a couple at the main table that morning. Thought they would come in handy. And I knew in my heart that Winnie would win the contest, so I thought they might give us bragging rights after the fact. Cute color, right?"

"Right. Yes." Janice gave the pad a closer look. Same shade of pink. Same narrow lines. "And you wrote the grocery list on this pad?"

"Yesterday."

Their conversation was interrupted when Taylor popped his head in the kitchen door.

"Just wanted to let you know Kip is here with some things Thorn ordered from the hardware store. I asked him to wait in the lobby."

"Kip?" Janice gathered her thoughts. "Oh, yes." The delivery boy from Vance Hardware. "Tell him I'll be right out."

"Fine, but he specifically asked for Georgia."

Everyone turned to look at Georgia, who blushed.

"I, well, I have no idea why he would ask for me. We only just met at the competition. I haven't talked to him for more than a few minutes."

Taylor shrugged. "He specifically asked for you."

Georgia's eyes widened. She untied her apron and ran her fingers through her hair.

Tess wiped her hands, and she and Janice followed Georgia to the lobby, where they found the handsome young delivery man holding two bags filled with supplies. His face lit up the moment he saw Georgia.

"Hey, just wanted to drop off these things that Thorn ordered."

"That was nice of you." Georgia reached out to take the bags.

"No problem." He flashed a warm smile, his gaze locked on Georgia. "I was out making another delivery anyway. Thorn is probably wondering why I didn't get here sooner."

"Thorn hasn't arrived yet," Janice explained. "So, no worries. You made it in plenty of time."

"Good." Kip glanced Janice's way then turned back to Georgia. "I almost didn't make it at all because of that dog."

"Are you talking about Huck?" Tess asked. "Did he get outside again?"

Kip shook his head and ran his fingers through his short hair. "No, some other dog. Scrawny little thing. Caked in mud too. Almost tripped over him on my way in. Could've killed myself."

As if on cue, Thorn barreled through the front door. He slammed the door behind him and then leaned against it. "When did you get another dog?"

"We didn't," Janice said. "The only dog around here, to my knowledge, is Huck."

Thorn shook his head. "Then you've got a stray on your hands."

"Really? I love dogs." Georgia bounded out the front door. Janice and Tess followed her onto the front walkway. Thorn and Kip came too.

No sooner did they step outside than a little short-haired dog ran toward them, tail wagging. Janice couldn't tell the breed at first glance, but the little fellow's tan hair was sure dirty. And boy, was he ever hyper. The dog leaped up and down like a yo-yo.

"Definitely looks like a stray," Thorn said.

Kip reached down to pet him, and the dog responded by trying to jump into his arms. "Told you he was kind of scrawny."

"Kind of?" Georgia's eyes brimmed over with tears as she knelt down next to the pooch. "Poor little guy. His ribs are sticking through. Looks like he hasn't had a good meal in weeks."

Thorn pointed to the dog. "If you feed that mongrel, he'll never go away. Besides, you've already got a dog and a cat. One more animal, and you'll have to start calling yourselves an inn for pets, not humans." Thorn put his hand up in the air. "I vote for taking him to the pound. All in favor, say aye."

Janice wasn't sure how to respond. It seemed a shame to send such an innocent little thing to the pound, where he might be euthanized. Still, she knew they couldn't keep him. They had their hands full already.

"But you know what happens at those places," Georgia pleaded.

Tess spoke up, her voice firm. "They give them baths, feed them, and then try to find good homes for them."

"Sometimes." Kip reached over to take the dog into his arms. "But if the shelter is overcrowded—and they always are— then older dogs like this don't stand a chance. If they aren't claimed or adopted within a few days, they're put down. Pretty sure that's what will happen to this little guy. I would suggest taking him to a vet to see if he's microchipped. Could be there's an owner looking for him. If not, we can go from there."

"Right. But that doesn't change the fact that we don't need—or want—another dog underfoot." Tess shook her head. "It's just not possible. And how do we know he doesn't have some sort of disease? We don't want to risk it with our own animals around. Not to mention our guests."

All eyes shifted to the pooch, whose tail thumped against Kip's arm and whose eyes gazed lovingly at Georgia. The young woman took him from Kip and spoke tenderly to him, her eyes misted with tears.

"You deserve a good home," she said as the little pooch responded to her touch. "I just can't bear the idea that you might end up at the pound." She stared at Tess and Janice, as if willing them to bend to her will.

Janice knew better, of course. The very last thing Tess would agree to was another dog in the inn. Even one as cute as this one. And she had to agree that the last thing they needed right now was another complication.

CHAPTER SEVEN

I'll take the dog," Kip reached over to scratch the dirty pup behind the ears. "I can't keep him for long, but I could get him cleaned up and take him to the vet to be checked out. If it turns out he has an owner, great. If not, maybe you ladies could help find him a home."

"God bless you, Kip!" Georgia cradled the pup in her arms and gave him a kiss on the top of the head.

Kip's cheeks flamed red, but he didn't seem to mind her joyous outburst. "It's okay. I don't mind. A few days won't hurt…until we find him a permanent home." He patted the pup again. "Cute little thing."

"Awfully dirty, though," Thorn said. "And the breed is a mystery. Not sure what you'd call a dog like that, anyway."

They all watched the spunky little guy, whose tail wagged in obvious thanks for their kindness.

Kip shrugged. "Maybe the vet will know. I'm guessing he's some sort of Chihuahua mix."

"Which would explain the high-pitched bark." Thorn put his fingers in his ears as the little yapper started a series of happy yips. When he calmed down, Thorn looked Kip's way. "Hey, I thought you were bringing my order."

"I did." Kip never shifted his gaze from Georgia and the dog. "It's inside on the front table."

"Okay. Thanks." Thorn headed inside to begin his work.

"Guess I'd better be going too," Kip said. "They'll wonder what's taking me so long."

Georgia passed the dog into Kip's arms and gave it another pat on the head.

As soon as Kip left with the little dog, Georgia looked Janice's way.

"Kip seems nice."

"Yes, very."

"Do you know him well?"

Beads of sweat rolled down Janice's back as the intense August heat got the better of her. "Pretty well. He works at Vance's Hardware and also catches a few hours as a waiter." She raised her eyebrows at Tess and added a teasing note to her voice. "Why do you ask?"

"Oh, no reason." A smile crept across Georgia's face. "Just wondering if he comes by a lot."

"Not a lot. Probably just being kind to Thorn, saving him a trip to the store."

"Probably." Georgia's lips curled up in a lovely smile.

"Let's get back inside. I'm about to melt into the pavement out here."

"It is awfully hot," Georgia agreed.

The women walked back into the inn, and Janice followed Georgia into the kitchen. The young woman settled back down to work, but she seemed a little distracted. Janice's thoughts shifted back to the pink writing tablet, and she was reminded that she needed to give the grocery list to Tess.

As she headed toward the lobby, paper in hand, Janice couldn't stop thinking about the Rising Star logo at the top. Georgia had admitted to getting the tablets from the competition. Was she the one who had put the slips of paper in the bread loaves, perhaps? Was she working with Sandie Ballard to make Winnie look bad? If so, why? She didn't seem to be the sort to want to hurt anyone. Then again, appearances could be deceiving. This Janice had learned the hard way over the past few months.

"Stop it, Janice," she said aloud. "You're imagining things."

"What are you imagining?" LuAnn appeared in the hallway. "Did you think you saw a mouse?"

"No. Why would you say that?"

"Thorn told me he found a dead one in that trap we set in the basement. Hauled it out to the Dumpster just this morning."

"Ick. I wish I didn't know that."

"Guess there's no untelling you now." LuAnn grinned. "But what are you imagining?"

She shrugged. "Nothing, really. Just pondering a few things."

They located Tess in the lobby visiting with Reena.

"Hey, Tess. Would you mind swinging by the grocery store and dropping off this list?" Janice asked.

"Don't mind a bit. I was just about to head out, so your timing is perfect." Tess turned to Reena. "Would you like to go for a little walk with me? It's a pretty day out."

"No, thanks. Too hot for me." Reena rose and walked to the elevator to go back up to her room. What she did up there, hour after hour, was a mystery to Janice, but who was she to question their guests? Maybe the woman just needed a nap. Or maybe, as Janice was beginning to suspect, dementia was stealing her days away.

After Tess left, LuAnn and Janice helped clear the café, then plopped down in armchairs in the library area. Janice was half-asleep when Tess got back from the store a short time later.

"Wake up, sleepyheads." Tess laughed. "So, this is what the mice do when the cat's away. They sleep."

"Mm-hmm." Janice yawned and stretched. "But please don't talk about mice. Not on a day when we trapped one."

"What would you think about taking a walk by the river?" Tess asked. "If we want to, we should head out before it gets too much hotter out there."

"We were out front with Kip and Georgia earlier and nearly melted into the sidewalk." Janice yawned again.

"What was Kip doing here?" LuAnn asked.

"Making a delivery. I'm just glad he's taking the dog."

LuAnn looked confused. "Wait, he's taking Huck?"

Janice chuckled. "No, the other dog. The little mongrel who showed up at our front door this morning."

"Wow. I haven't had the pleasure of meeting him."

"Hopefully you won't have to." Janice pushed her chair back. "Hey, do you both have a minute? I want to run something by you." When the others nodded, she stood. "Hold tight. I'll be right back." She took off toward the kitchen and returned with the Rising Star writing tablet. Janice held it up in Tess and LuAnn's direction. "Georgia picked up a few of these tablets at the competition."

"Oh, they're cute." LuAnn gave the tablet a closer look.

"Yes, very," Janice agreed. "But did you notice it's the same paper the laminated messages were written on?"

"Whoa. Well, now that you mention it…" Tess took the tablet and gave it a closer look.

"See the pink and white swirls just under the surface? The paper is textured too."

"Rising Star was giving them away?" LuAnn asked. "Anyone could have taken them, I guess."

"Yes, but I can't stop thinking about Georgia. We know she had access to the tablets and that she used one for this week's grocery list."

"Yes, but, really, anyone at the inn would have access."

"That's true." Janice paused. "But let's think about it for a minute. What do we really know about Georgia, other than the fact that she seemed keen on staying with Winnie for a month and learning her baking secrets?"

"But if you recall," Tess interjected, "her parents were on board with the idea too. They were all smitten with Winnie's cooking."

"Yes. I just wish we knew more about her. All we know is that she was born and raised in Akron."

"She's very pretty," Tess added. "She's got that porcelain skin that's so lovely, just perfect with those dark brown curls. And those eyes…wow. Does she wear contacts?"

"No, I heard her telling Winnie they've been bright blue like that from the time she was teensy-tiny. She gets lots of compliments on them."

"Well, we can all agree that she's beautiful, and I also think her reasons for being here are legitimate," Tess said. "But if I see any suspicious behavior, I promise to let you know."

The friends wrapped up their conversation, and Tess talked Janice into taking a walk with her. Just as they were about to open the front door to step outside, the local florist, Katrina Kingston, entered in a rush with a half-loaf of bread in her hands.

"Uh-oh." Janice didn't mean to say it out loud but couldn't help herself. Looked like they had another tainted loaf.

"Who do I need to talk to about this bread?" Katrina shoved the bread Janice's way. "Yes. It tastes fine—good, even—but that weird note inside really gave me the creeps. Are you guys doing some sort of Halloween prank a couple of months early?"

"No." Janice did her best not to groan aloud. "Would you mind telling me what the note said?"

"It said I should cancel my reservation or something terrible would happen to my family."

Ugh. This just kept getting worse and worse.

"If this is a marketing stunt to get more attention, I don't think it's a very good one." Katrina looked back and forth between Janice and Tess. "But I'm guessing it's not."

"I can promise you, it is not." Tess took the loaf of bread from Janice's hands and looked it over. "Did you bring the note?"

"Yes." Katrina fished in her jeans pocket and handed Janice the note. Pink paper. Laminated. Sloppy handwriting.

"Right." Janice truly didn't know what else to say, so she simply said, "We're so sorry about this, and we're happy to replace the loaf of bread. Winnie has talked about doing more baking, so we can get you a fresh loaf soon as a thank-you for booking with us."

"No thanks." Katrina shook her head. "And I'm not really comfortable with my mom and dad staying here, what with a threat like that. Especially if you don't know who's making it. It could be some crazy serial killer or something. Please go ahead and cancel their reservation."

"Of course, Katrina. We'll do that." Janice apologized once again, then watched as the woman turned and walked out of the building.

"If this keeps up, we'll lose all the reservations we just got." Tess continued to stare at the loaf of bread, as if it might explode in her hands.

Janice was worried about that very thing. But, at the moment, she was also worried about something else. The only other person helping Winnie with the baking was Georgia. The young woman seemed innocent enough, but perhaps she had secrets yet uncovered, secrets that involved Sandie Ballard.

Maybe Georgia Hauser was here to learn how to cook...or maybe she wasn't. Perhaps, like Kylie, she had come to Wayfarers Inn with ulterior motives. Janice would have to keep a very close eye on the young woman.

CHAPTER EIGHT

August 4, 1860

Prudence stared at the injured man in disbelief. Could he be a Friend? Her mind whirled. His speech had an unmistakable drawl to it, but his use of plain speech overrode her fears. She pulled a chair out from the table and sat across from him.

The man reached his good hand to her, and the smile never left his face. "I mean thee no harm, truly. I have traveled from Kentucky these past six days and am halfway to my destination. I am here in good faith."

She gave the man a closer look. His clothes, mud-covered and torn as they were, were finely made and of rich material. There were lines of pain around his mouth, but his eyes were clear and steady.

"I ask thy forgiveness, ma'am, for my appearance." He looked down at his bloodied arm and grimaced. "And for coming into thy kitchen in such a way. My name is William."

"What has happened to thee, William?" Prudence blurted. "Did thee fall from thy horse?"

"In a manner of speaking, yes, I did. I was waylaid about five miles back by a man intent on first beating me and then robbing me." He took a deep breath. "By the grace of God, another man came along who overpowered the ruffian, and I was able to retain my goods and my horse."

Prudence gazed into his dark eyes and tried to make sense of this. "But why come here?"

William touched his temple, and Prudence noticed for the first time that there was dried blood clotted there. "After I told my story to the man who helped me, he told me I should go to Riverfront House. He said there was a woman who ran the kitchen there who would help me. That I should tether my horse in the woods and come to the inn on foot."

Prudence stood. "Before we go any further, my name is Prudence. I am going to tend thy wounds. Thee should sit and rest for a bit."

While the water heated on the stove, Prudence gathered clean cloths and witch hazel. By the time she turned to tend William, he had fallen asleep, with his head supported by his good arm. She let him sleep for a while until she got the dishes washed and the bread in the oven and then gently woke him and cleaned the wounds on his arm and temple, binding them with the cloths. William dozed a bit more while she set the bread to cool and finished cleaning the kitchen.

She woke him once more and helped him stand. "Let us get thee on thy feet. Thee will come with me to my house, where thee will spend the night. My husband, Jason, will fetch thy horse for thee."

William looked at her, openmouthed. "But thee doesn't know anything about me. Why would thee bring a stranger from the South into thy home?"

"Thee is a Friend," Prudence said simply. "Thee is injured and in need of help. That is enough."

CHAPTER NINE

Late Wednesday night, Janice tossed and turned in her bed. Ordinarily, she slept like a baby in her lovely room on the fourth floor of Wayfarers Inn. Tonight, however, sleep eluded her. She couldn't stop thinking about the goings-on over the past couple of days, starting with the revelation of the messages in the loaves of bread. Who would want to sabotage Winnie? What sort of person would stoop to such a level? And...why? Talk about a strange way to make a statement.

Poor Winnie. Up one minute—winner of the Rising Star competition—and down the next. And on top of the emotional toll this was taking on her, Winnie seemed to be struggling physically. On more than one occasion, Janice noticed her hobbling on that bad knee.

Something needed to give, and soon. Maybe they really should involve the police. Perhaps tomorrow she could call Officer Randy Lewis. Something had to be done about this, especially with so many different notes floating around out there. And what if others showed up? Then what? The Inn Crowd would have some explaining to do. Only, as of yet, they were still reeling from the shock of it all.

She heard a growl, followed by a bark. Something had Huck worked up again tonight. Probably a car driving by. A couple of minutes later, Janice relaxed and willed herself to doze off. Just as twilight sleep set in, a slight vibration roused her once again.

The elevator.

But who used the elevator at midnight? Tess and LuAnn wouldn't be roaming around the inn at this hour unless there was some sort of emergency.

Very faintly, she heard a groan. Someone was in pain. Another round of barking from Huck propelled her from bed. Janice reached for her robe, slipped it on, and tiptoed to the door. She was met in the hall by Tess.

"You heard it too?"

Janice nodded.

Tess held up a flashlight and whispered, "Just in case."

Janice tied the belt on her robe into a neat loop. "In case you need to knock a burglar senseless, you've brought a flashlight?"

"No, silly. We just need to be able to see. The last thing we need is one of us tumbling down the stairs in the dark."

"True, that."

Tess waved her flashlight. "Not sure I'd be brave enough to go down on my own, but if you're willing to come, I say we scope out the place, just to make sure nothing's amiss."

Janice reluctantly agreed. Tess led the way to the stairs, the low beam of her little flashlight reflecting on the wall, casting eerie shadows. About halfway down, one of the stairs creaked. Janice made the rest of the journey on tiptoe, not wanting to alert any would-be bad guys. On the other hand, maybe they should make a lot of noise so any burglars would take off before she met them face-to-face.

When they reached the third floor, they heard the elevator door open down below. Tess put her finger to her lips and turned off her flashlight. The time for true bravery had come.

They eased their way down, one quiet step at a time. Janice clung tight to the rail and willed herself not to stumble.

When they got to the landing between the first and second floors, a shadow moved below them in the lobby. There was just enough light from the lamp they left on at night in the lobby to make out the culprit. Reena Newberry. But why was she awake at midnight? She usually went to her room hours before everyone else. And why creep downstairs in the night?

The tiny woman's shadow danced across the wall as she passed by the lamp. Her usually perfect white hair stood up straight atop her head, as if she'd had an electric shock. Janice couldn't quite make out the robe to tell its color, but the buttons were all cockeyed, as if she'd done them up in her sleep or in the dark. Very odd.

Janice's thoughts began to twist and turn. Maybe Reena was confused or even walking in her sleep. She could very likely end up hurting herself. Janice wondered if she should call out Reena's name and run the risk of startling her. That might make things worse instead of better. Perhaps they should just keep trailing her until a solution presented itself.

They started down the last set of stairs. "What in the world?" Tess's words came out in a hoarse whisper as a stair creaked under her foot. "We really need to get this step fixed," she added.

"Shh!" Janice's pulse quickened as they tiptoed about twenty feet behind Reena. She couldn't help but wonder where the older woman was headed.

Beneath Janice's feet, another loose floorboard creaked. Reena turned around, and for a moment Janice felt sure she had seen them. Only when the elderly woman turned back and continued on her way did Janice breathe a sigh of relief.

Janice and Tess eased their way down the hall, careful to keep some distance between Reena and themselves. Janice watched as she slipped into the kitchen, a blithe spirit, like a shadow slipping past the moon. For a moment, she wondered if she'd seen Reena at all. The woman came and went like a flash after a photograph.

"I feel like I'm in Oz," she whispered. "People come and go so quickly around here."

Whatever had propelled Reena to go to the kitchen in the middle of the night? Surely she knew that guests weren't allowed in there.

Janice's heart thumped with extra oomph as she and Tess inched their way toward the kitchen door. Once there, they watched from the hallway as Reena tiptoed past the counter. She reached down for something on the countertop. Janice could barely make it out. Only the tiny light above the stove gave any indication of what Reena might have taken into her hand.

A Rising Star note tablet.

Now why would Reena need a writing tablet in the middle of the night?

Before Janice could come up with any answers, Reena eased her way toward the pantry, her plush slippers moving along the kitchen floor in silence. Moments later she came out with something else in her hand that Janice couldn't quite make out. A snack, maybe? The elderly woman turned toward them. Janice and Tess skedaddled toward the stairs. A couple of minutes later, they arrived, breathless, on the fourth floor.

"Well, that was odd," Tess said.

"You can say that twice and mean it." Janice shook her head. "Very peculiar. And it sure raises a lot of questions in my mind. What in the world is she up to?"

"I don't know. I'm actually more worried that she's suffering from dementia and doesn't have a clue what she's doing herself."

"I thought about that too." Janice yawned. "But I vote we talk about this in the morning. It's been a long day already."

"I agree." Tess said good night just as the hum of the elevator started again. Reena must be headed back to her room.

Janice did the same. She walked into the comfort of her room, did her best to put the whole thing out of her mind, and crawled back in bed for what she hoped would be a good night's sleep. Unfortunately, she didn't sleep well at all. In fact, she returned to tossing and turning, and when she did finally doze, her sleep was fitful, at best.

The following morning Janice and Tess relayed the events of the night before to LuAnn over breakfast in the kitchen.

LuAnn took a sip of her orange juice and leaned back in her chair. "I can't believe I slept through the whole thing. Then again, I was exhausted after the excitement of yesterday. And I took a melatonin tablet. They're very helpful for sleep."

"I wish I'd thought of that. I barely slept at all." Janice fought a yawn. "So, what do you think Reena was doing in the kitchen?"

Tess shrugged. "We know for sure she swiped a pad of that pink paper from the competition."

"And something else from the pantry, but I couldn't make it out in the dark," Janice added. "I'm guessing a cookie. She loves Winnie's cookies."

"I can understand about the cookies. She does have a particular penchant for those. But maybe it's not all that strange about the notepad." LuAnn didn't seem quite as concerned. "Maybe she just needed to write a note and needed paper."

Tess shook her head. "There's no way of knowing unless we ask her, and I don't plan to do that."

"Me neither," Janice agreed. "And if she was writing a note in the night, maybe it was some sort of complaint against one of us. Maybe we've yet to see it because she hasn't come downstairs yet."

"That's a possibility." LuAnn didn't look like she cared for this explanation at all. "Tell me what she was wearing."

"A bathrobe." Tess took a bite of her eggs, then reached for her toast.

"I presume a nightgown underneath," Janice added. "Why do you ask?"

"I was just curious if she was already dressed for bed or if she was still in street clothes, which might indicate a planned outing."

"Definitely a robe." Janice paused to think about it. "But then again, she could have been wearing street clothes underneath. Maybe the robe was just a ruse, to throw us off."

LuAnn took a sip of her coffee. "Do you think she saw you?"

"No." Janice shook her head. "I don't think so, anyway. But maybe she was going somewhere and put on the robe in case anyone caught her up and about. That way she could easily use the 'midnight snack' excuse."

LuAnn set her mug on the table. "If she didn't see you and had clothes on underneath her robe, then she would have left the inn. So, either she saw you and went to the kitchen to fool you, or she had nightclothes on under the robe and meant to go the kitchen all along."

Winnie buzzed through the room with a tray of cookies in hand. "Sorry to interrupt, but speaking of midnight snacks, I made snickerdoodles before I left yesterday." She gestured to the tray. "I put them in the pantry. Did you get one? I'm about to put the rest out at the front desk."

"No." Janice bit back a yawn as she reached for one of Winnie's delicious cinnamon sugar cookies. "I wish I'd known before I headed to bed. I would've taken a couple up with me. I couldn't sleep."

Winnie gave her a sympathetic look. "Sorry to hear that. I told Reena yesterday afternoon before I left that she could help herself to the cookies on the tray in the café."

Tess pressed her palms against the table. "Well, for goodness' sake, why didn't you tell us?" she said crossly.

"I did." Winnie shrugged and grabbed a cookie. "Just now." She took a bite and headed toward the lobby.

Janice chuckled. "So, there you have it. Reena was simply coming downstairs for a midnight snack. But I don't know why she ended up in the kitchen instead of the café. Probably just confused, which further deepens my suspicions about her memory."

"So it would seem." LuAnn released a slow breath. "But something about the whole thing still seems odd to me. Why take the pad of pink paper?"

"No idea." Tess dabbed at her lips with a napkin. "Strange, for sure."

Georgia headed toward them, her brow wrinkled in obvious concern. "I'm afraid to tell Winnie this, but we're missing some cookies that were in the pantry."

"We have a suspect in mind," Tess said. "Just trust us on this one."

When Georgia looked perplexed, Tess added, "Reena Newberry. We caught her going into the kitchen last night. It was so odd."

"Everything about the woman is odd." Robin's voice sounded from behind them. They turned to face her. "She asked me not to clean her room again yesterday. Don't you find that strange?"

Janice shrugged. "I suppose she has a right to keep the room any way she likes it while she's staying here."

"Up to a point," Tess interrupted. "If she's taking food in there, we could end up with ants. Or worse."

"I've seen roaches the size of rats," Robin said.

"In the inn?" Tess's eyes widened.

"No, down by the river. I'm just saying we don't want to attract them."

"Right." Janice shuddered.

Robin lowered her voice, as if expecting Reena to appear at any moment. "I just get the feeling she's hiding something, that's all."

"She is," Tess whispered back. "A snickerdoodle and a writing tablet."

"Yes, don't forget that," Janice said. "It might turn out to be a critical piece of evidence."

"I think we should keep an eye on her." Robin pulled up a chair and sat down. "Ever since she arrived, I've had the weirdest feeling she was up to something. Otherwise, why not let me change the sheets or at least make the bed? She's been with us three nights now."

"I peeked in the room yesterday, and the bed was made," LuAnn said. "In fact, the entire room was impeccably clean. Not a thing out of place."

"Guess that explains it," Tess said. "She's her own maid."

"Some people just have the gift of cleanliness, I guess." Janice paused to think through her next words. "And if I had to guess, I'd say she's nervous about letting someone else clean the room because she's got all of that expensive jewelry in there. Remember? She told us about it when she arrived."

"I offered to put it in the safe," LuAnn countered. "She wouldn't hear of it."

"Maybe, but I'd still be nervous if I had thousands of dollars' worth of property tucked away in my room. You know?"

"I guess."

"And did you see that ensemble Reena was wearing yesterday?" Robin's eyes widened. "Wowza. That woman's got some money."

"Maybe she's the sort who just looks rich but really isn't." LuAnn shrugged.

"No, she's the real deal." Janice stopped to reflect. "Those rings she's wearing are worth thousands. And I saw her carrying a Gucci handbag. Those things are unbelievably expensive. She's got money, all right."

"For someone who's well off, she seems cranky most of the time," Tess observed. "Just proves the old adage that money can't buy happiness."

"I've noticed that too." Janice paused to think before adding any other thoughts. "You know, I've decided that aging makes you more of what you already are. Most of the golden years folks I know are either very cranky or very sweet. I guess a lot of it depends on what you've been through in your life."

"I'd say it has more to do with how you respond to the events that have happened in your life," LuAnn said. "We can't control the things that happen to us, but we can control our responses."

"Good point." Janice pondered her friend's words. "There's more to Reena Newberry than meets the eye. She's been here for days with no apparent reason for coming in the first place."

"True." Tess nodded. "We rarely have guests stay this long during the week unless there's a big family event going on or something like that. She's had no visitors. And yet every day she dresses up, as if she's expecting someone."

"What brought her to Marietta?" Janice asked. "Is she in town for a wedding? A family gathering?"

"Some folks come just to sightsee." LuAnn bit into her toast.

Janice gave her a knowing look. "But that's just it…she rarely leaves the inn. She's been here four days, and I've hardly seen her 'do' anything except meander from room to room and complain about our service."

LuAnn's eyes widened. "Oh my goodness. You don't suppose she's another reviewer, do you? Maybe she's just here to watch how we perform, then she'll rate us in some magazine."

Janice couldn't imagine that. "I guess that's possible, but why choose someone so advanced in age? Wouldn't a reviewer work for someone?"

"Our competition, perhaps?"

"But she's from Pennsylvania. Let's say she does work for— or even owns—a competitive inn. It wouldn't be in Marietta."

"Right." LuAnn sighed. "You've got me. I don't know why she's here."

Winnie passed back through the room, tray now empty. "Did it ever occur to any of you that she just came here to get away from things for a while? You've been marketing the inn all over the place, in a variety of publications and even on the web. Let's just say your marketing worked. She saw an ad for the place, decided she needed a getaway, and—"

"Hired a driver to bring her from Pennsylvania just to spend a few sweltering days in Marietta?" Janice shrugged. "I guess it's possible."

"When you put it like that, it does make me wonder what she's getting away from." Tess seemed to lose herself to her thoughts. "What did she leave behind in Pennsylvania?"

"Likely a huge house filled with keepsakes from years gone by, including a photo album with pictures of the husband she lost a few years back and kids and grandkids who are too busy to pay her a visit." Winnie tied an apron around her waist and walked toward the stove. "Now, if you don't mind, I'm going to fire up Big Red and get started on lunch so everyone—including Reena Newberry—has food to eat. Otherwise you really will get some bad reviews for the inn."

Janice thought about Winnie's words for some time as she tidied up the café in preparation for the lunch crowd. She couldn't shake the notion that Reena Newberry had come to the inn for more than a simple vacation. Something had propelled her here…but, what? Or who?

CHAPTER TEN

After tidying up the café, Janice went in search of the newspaper. Hopefully she could read Hank Clive's article before anyone else got to it. Strangely, she couldn't seem to find a copy. The entire lobby container was empty, in fact. That never happened this early in the day.

Around ten forty-five, she noticed Reena ambling toward the café. The woman was definitely a late sleeper. Or maybe it just took her a while to pull together such a fashionable look. Her hair and makeup were done, and she certainly looked as vibrant as ever in a bright pink floral blouse and capris ensemble.

Janice couldn't help but notice that Reena was hobbling more than usual. That might have something to do with the stylish sandals. Maybe they were pinching her feet. As she moved through the parlor, Reena let out a couple of quiet groans.

"Are you all right, Reena?"

The elderly woman paused and rubbed her left leg. "I banged my knee against the elevator door last night. Hurts like the dickens."

"The elevator door?" Perhaps Reena would open up and confess her midnight trip to the kitchen.

Instead, she nodded and mumbled, "Clumsy oaf. I need to watch where I'm going."

And not try to maneuver the elevator in the dark, Janice wanted to add, but didn't. Instead she opted for, "If you feel you need medical attention, please let me know. I'll be happy to call the doctor for you."

"Doctor-schmoctor." With a huff, Reena settled into a chair at the closest table. "But a cup of coffee would go a long way in helping me heal. Two sugars, and don't scrimp on the cream. That server yesterday was stingy with my cream. I told her that coffee should be the color of caramel, but did she listen? No, she did not."

"Two sugars, plenty of cream." Janice smiled and turned toward the kitchen.

As she walked into the room, the familiar aroma of peanut soup filled the air. Janice breathed it in, thankful, as always, for Winnie's presence in the kitchen. She found her friend up to her elbows in soup kettles with LuAnn and Georgia helping.

Winnie stopped stirring and narrowed her eyes. "Let me guess…that's for Miss I've-got-to-have-more-cream-than-everybody-else?"

"Yes." Janice smiled. "She is a bit needy."

LuAnn looked at Janice. "I still say she's up to something, Don't you find it odd that she showed up on the very day the loaves of bread were tampered with?"

"I never saw her in my kitchen," Winnie argued. "I would've shooed her right out."

"And yet, she seemed to know her way around the kitchen last night when she snuck down for a treat." Janice snapped her fingers. "I just remembered something. I heard Huck barking on Monday night after I went up to my room. Maybe she was on the prowl then, like she was last night. She could have come down to the kitchen to put those notes in the bread without any of us realizing."

"That would mean she came all the way from Pennsylvania prepared for such a task," LuAnn countered. "Why would she do that? We don't even know her."

"I have no idea." Janice chewed on the inside of her lip as she considered the possibilities. "But we can't deny the fact that she had access on Monday night, and her whole demeanor changed during that same time period."

"True." LuAnn shrugged. "I just wish I knew more about her."

"Do you think a bit of sleuthing is in order?" Janice asked. "She's in the café right now, so this is an excellent time to head up to her room to clean."

"I thought she asked for her room to be left alone," LuAnn said.

Janice shrugged. "We can only go so long without cleaning a guest's room. So, what do you say? I'll swing by her table and ask if she would like a change of sheets."

"I guess so." LuAnn didn't look terribly enthusiastic about the notion though.

Janice delivered the coffee to Reena in the café. "Reena, I know you've declined housekeeping services, but how about we just go up and give you a fresh change of sheets?"

For a second, Reena looked like she wanted to protest, but then she nodded. "Yes, I suppose some clean sheets would be nice. But please, don't do anything else."

"We'll be careful," Janice said. She summoned LuAnn from the kitchen and Tess from the office, and the three made their way up to the third floor to Sunshine and Daisies.

LuAnn opened the door, and the three women stepped inside what turned out to be a spotless room.

"Well, there you go." Tess gestured around the room. "She really is tidy."

"She did say to just change the sheets." Janice walked over to the bed and pulled back the comforter, revealing the sheets below. Tess walked to the other side of the bed and helped her toss the pillows onto the chair in the corner. As she did, a velvet bag slipped out from its hiding place under a pillow and fell onto the floor below. Several items of jewelry spilled from its opening.

"Ack. Let me get that." Tess leaned down and came up with the bag and the loose jewelry. She spread the items on the bed. "Looks like a pearl necklace, a couple of brooches, some jade earrings, and a ring." She placed the jewelry back in the bag and set it aside.

LuAnn and Janice continued to remove the sheets, which they tossed onto the floor. Then they remade the bed, and Tess tucked the velvet bag under the pillow.

Janice walked around the bed to fetch the dirty sheets. LuAnn turned to walk to the door but paused and pointed to an envelope on the dresser. "Hey, I think I've just figured out why Reena is in Marietta. Check this out."

Janice and Tess walked over to have a look. The envelope was open, and a portion of the paper inside could be seen. Janice read the words, "You are cordially invited..." at the top of the gray sheet of paper, then turned her attention elsewhere.

"Now we've gone to snooping. I say we get out of here. I think we can safely conclude that Reena is here to attend some sort of upcoming function." She pointed to the nightstand, which held a small plate with cookies on it. "We'll leave those as well. She told us just to change the sheets, and I intend to honor that."

"Agreed," LuAnn said. The ladies gathered up the dirty sheets and walked toward the door.

Janice reached to close the closet door, which was standing ajar, but something inside caught her eye. There, on top of Reena's suitcase, sat the pink pad of paper. It didn't appear to be written on.

Janice closed the door and put it out of her mind. She followed behind the other ladies to the stairway, then carried the sheets down to the laundry room and put them in the washer. Then she went back upstairs. Georgia headed her way with a newspaper under her arm. She had a concerned expression on her face. She gave Janice a wide-eyed look and whispered, "Hide this after you read the article about Winnie," then passed the newspaper into her hands.

Janice slipped into the lobby to read the article. It turned out Hank Clive was a stellar reporter. He certainly kept his ear to the ground. He'd heard about the threatening notes. He hadn't missed a beat with his more-than-thorough article about the messages in the bread. The piece read more like a work of investigative journaling than a local feature story about a star baker. Ugh. But, how would the people of Marietta respond? Would they be scared off, or intrigued? Maybe this story would add to the inn's already-fascinating ambiance.

Tess entered the room with a copy of the paper in her hand. "Did you read it?"

"Just." Janice did her best not to sigh aloud.

"He's trying to make us look bad."

"He's just doing what reporters do," Janice countered. "Going to print with a juicy story."

"Well, this is one juicy story I'd rather see disappear. Publicity is always nice, but not this sort." Tess sighed and tossed the paper into the trash can. "I emptied the container of papers and hid them all in my room."

"I wondered what happened to them. I was afraid there'd been a run on newspapers."

"Nope. I just didn't want the guests to stumble across that article."

"Thank you. Heaven forbid Reena should read it."

"Read what?" LuAnn joined them at the foot of the stairs. "Oh, Winnie's article! It came out today, right?"

"Right, but LuAnn, I think I should warn you that—"

"I still can't believe Winnie got her very own story. She could stand a little pick-me-up this morning, after what she's been through over the past few days."

Knock-me-down would be more like it. Janice wanted to say the words aloud, but didn't. She turned to face LuAnn. "If you want to read it, the nearest one is in the trash bin in the lobby."

"That bad?"

"Mm-hmm." Janice led the way, and before long, LuAnn had a copy of the paper in her hands—somewhat sticky after someone had tossed a half-eaten blueberry muffin on top of it.

LuAnn brushed her sticky fingers against her slacks and groaned. "Let's go into the café and sit down, shall we?"

"No!" Tess and Janice said simultaneously.

"Someone might see us," Janice added.

Janice led the way to the unoccupied library area of the lobby, and she and Tess waited while LuAnn read the article.

"Oh, my goodness." LuAnn clasped a hand over her mouth and pulled it back down, eyes now bugging. "Winnie is going to be so hurt."

"Yes, which is why we're hoping she forgets that Hank Clive was ever doing an article in the first place," Janice said.

LuAnn squinted. "Well, now that you bring it up, I've only met the man a couple of times, but I can tell you that something about him doesn't sit well with me."

"Me too," Janice acknowledged.

"I'm not just talking about his article," LuAnn added. "Even before that, I had my suspicions. That first day when he barreled in here with all of his equipment, it was almost like he was taking over the place."

"And he was getting a little too friendly with our guests too," Janice added. "Reena told me that he asked to take photos of the rooms on her floor."

Tess groaned. "I hope she said no."

Janice responded with a nod. "I don't want to criticize the man. I don't even know him. But he certainly took advantage of this situation to make us all look bad."

"He definitely didn't make a very good impression on any of us," Tess agreed. "I know he's new in town, but I don't remember hearing him say where he hailed from. Do you?"

"No, not at all." Janice paused to think about it. "Someplace south of here. He's got a distinctive Southern accent."

"Don't you remember?" LuAnn asked. "Brad said he came from Kentucky. But he doesn't seem like the big city type, so I don't think he's from one of the major papers. And he seemed a little hungry for the story, didn't he?"

"Definitely," Janice and Tess agreed.

Tess shrugged. "He's just doing what reporters do. He's not very old, so maybe this is his first job. And who knows? This could even be his first big story."

"Winnie is a pretty big story." LuAnn's eye took on a distant look. "One minute she's stirring peanut soup, the next she's a superstar."

"She's always been a star in my book," Janice said, "which is why I don't want to see her hurt. If anyone deserves to be well thought of, it's our Winnie."

"All of this is getting me so upset." Tess's cheeks flamed red. "I'm sorry we ever let that Hank Clive in the front door in the first place."

"Technically, he barged in and made himself at home," Janice reminded her.

Fine lines formed between Tess's eyes. "I'm just so worried Winnie will find out."

"Me too." LuAnn looked mortified by this suggestion. "You don't think she already knows, do you?"

Janice shook her head. "She hasn't mentioned anything, so I guess we're safe. I'm going to head back into the kitchen and help her with the lunch menu. She seems pretty worn out."

"No doubt," Tess said. "If I didn't have so much paperwork to do, I'd help out. But with all these bookings, I'm falling behind. And don't even get me started on Robin and Thorn. They came to me this morning with a list of things that need to be done. We'll all be worn out before long."

Janice gave her an encouraging smile. "At least things were picking up before the news broke about the messages in the bread. There is that. So hopefully folks will just forget about it, and things will go on as usual."

"Hopefully."

LuAnn tossed her paper into the trash, but Janice couldn't stop thinking about Hank's unflattering article. Hopefully Winnie would never see it.

She arrived in the kitchen to find Winnie and Robin in what appeared to be an argument.

"What's going on?" Janice asked.

"She's hiding a copy of the *Times* under her arm and won't let me see it." Winnie pointed at Robin.

Robin took a couple of steps backward, as if wanting to run away. "I, well, I . . . I can't, Winnie."

"And why not?" Winnie put her hands on her hips. "Hand over that paper, Robin, or there won't be any more snickerdoodles for you, today or any other day."

Robin's eyes widened, and she shoved the paper in Winnie's direction.

CHAPTER ELEVEN

Winnie flipped through the newspaper until she located the article. Janice held her breath as Winnie read in silence. When she finished, Winnie wadded up the paper and tossed it across the room toward the trash can. It landed on the floor.

"Well, how do you like them apples? Barely a mention of my win or my personal story. Just a hard hit from a man wanting to pin me to the wall for something I didn't even do. I'd hardly call that fair."

Taylor entered the kitchen, arms loaded down with a tray of dishes. "Who wants to pin you to the wall, Winnie?"

Winnie pointed to the newspaper on the floor. "Page four, third column, bottom right."

Taylor set the tray down, picked up the newspaper, then smoothed out the pages. He scanned until he found the article. He read it without saying a word. When he finished, he folded the paper neatly, laid it on the counter, and said, "Whoa."

"You can say that twice and mean it." Winnie reached for her ladle.

"What a jerk. Why's he making such a big deal about those notes in the bread?" Taylor asked. "Surely he knows we're not behind that."

"He just wants a story," Winnie said. "I told you that after my first encounter with him at the competition. He was backstage nosing around and making me nervous. You might recall, I mentioned my concerns that same day."

Janice remembered. "You were right, Winnie. I'm sorry we didn't pick up on it, or we would have protected you from this. But don't worry. I'm going to call Randy. Maybe he can help us get to the bottom of this."

Winnie looked mortified by this suggestion. "Officer Lewis? I wish you wouldn't. I'm already embarrassed enough."

"Are you sure? We might have no choice, if we can't figure this out ourselves."

Winnie gave her a knowing look. "You're the Inn Crowd. It's what you do."

Janice couldn't help but laugh. "Okay, we're on the case. But be prepared for intervention from the police department if we get stuck or if things become dangerous. I don't want anything to distract you from this upcoming competition."

"Well, speaking of the competition, I've only got a week and a half to get ready for the big one. I'm going to have to ignore the article in that paper and focus on my baking." Winnie used her hand towel as a fan. "If I can stand the heat. And I've made several fresh loaves of bread for folks who got bad ones before." She pointed at four loaves wrapped in plastic wrap on the counter. "At least we know these are okay. I baked them fresh this morning, and Georgia was with me for every minute of it."

"They look delicious," Janice said. "But I don't know how you do it, Winnie. You really need to slow down."

"If only I had time." Winnie's eyes widened, and her lips curled up in a smile. "I've got to be prepared for this upcoming competition, and that means focusing on new recipes. The bread category is pretty self-explanatory, but man, when it comes to pies—"

Robin interrupted her to tell a story about a pie her mother had once made for her—a total flop. On and on she went, talking about how her mom's attempt at chocolate cream pie looked more like a bowl of chocolate soup.

Winnie took control of the conversation once again as she led them through an animated list of potential pies one might see at the competition.

"I can't wait to see what you come up with," Georgia said as she emerged from the pantry. "You'll win that one, hands-down."

Winnie looked a little embarrassed by this flattery. "Remember, this is a statewide competition and includes all of the county winners. I'll be up against some of the best, so there's no guarantee."

"Poo. They've got nothing on you." Janice laughed at her unintended rhyme. "Anyway, this isn't about winning. It's about how you play the game."

"True. It'll be a memory to last forever. And a great way to bring attention to the inn too." Winnie shrugged and got back to work.

Janice went to Winnie and gave her a one-armed hug. "I appreciate you thinking of us, Winnie, but please don't make it about that anymore. Sure, we've benefitted from the attention you've received, but please forgive us if we ever made this contest about us. It's not. It's about you."

"Actually..." The edges of Winnie's lips curled up in a delicious smile. "It's about Him." She pointed up. "Whatever blessings the Lord showers down on me—whatever talents or abilities—I want to give them right back to Him, along with all the honor and praise."

Janice couldn't help but smile as she went back to the counter to write the names of the ones who should receive the bread on sticky notes and put them on the wrapped loaves. Leave it to Winnie to shift the focus to their Creator.

"You've got such a great attitude, Winnie." Georgia walked over to her and slipped her arm around Winnie's waist. "But I still say you'll win the pie category, hands down." She lavished Winnie with a hearty hug, then got right back to work.

This led to a rousing "Amen!" from everyone in the kitchen.

"I need to focus on growing my menu for the inn," Winnie said. "I've been thinking of adding more products that locals might enjoy, things we could sell out of the café. Not necessarily things folks would come here to eat, though. More... takeout."

"Takeout?" This confused Janice. "Sweets, you mean?"

"Well, here's an example." Suddenly Winnie was all business. "Local kids are going back to school soon."

"And?"

"I say we do some themed back-to-school cookies to sell."

"We're not running a bakery, Winnie. And aren't you already worn out?"

Winnie heaved a little sigh. "Okay, okay. I just found out that Sandie Ballard's new bakery has all sorts of things like that. I'm trying to keep up with the Joneses."

"Stop it." Janice put her hand up. "Seriously. You do you. Don't try to compete with Sandie Ballard or anyone else."

Janice couldn't help but notice that Georgia flinched as soon as Sandie Ballard's name was spoken. The young woman scooted out of the room, headed for the pantry. Strange.

Winnie plopped down into a chair and rested her elbows on the table. "That's so easy to say, but not at all easy to do."

"Stay focused on the prize, Winnie, and I don't mean the one at the state competition. God didn't call you to work at Sandie's bakery or to compete with her in any way."

Winnie offered up a half-hearted, "Okay."

Knowing she had said enough, Janice left the kitchen in search of Tess. She found her in the office, doing paperwork. Janice knocked on the open door and then cleared her throat.

"I hate to bother you, but…"

"Everything okay?" Tess asked.

Janice nodded. "Yes. But I think this competition thing is really getting to Winnie. She's worried about Sandie Ballard."

"I guess I can understand that. Sandie's got a lot going for her. But she's not our Winnie." Tess paused. "Hey, speaking of Sandie, I read an article in the paper about her new place. Sounds really nice."

"Don't mention it to Winnie, okay? She's already keen on turning the inn into a bakery, complete with themed cookies."

"Oh my. She's busy enough already."

"That's what I told her. I'm not sure why she's so bothered by a new bakery opening in town, but she is. It's almost like she has to prove that she can outdo the new gal."

"I'm sorry she feels that way. To be honest, we don't really know much about this new woman."

"Other than the fact that she calls her shop the Better Batter, which implies she thinks she's the best, I don't know much either." Janice shrugged. "But I'd like to find out, especially since she turned up at our back door and had a private meeting with Georgia."

"Right. We definitely need to learn more." Tess turned her attention to the computer in front of her. "That's why God invented the World Wide Web." She clicked a key and signed online. It didn't take long to find Sandie's bio on a site listing graduates from an expensive culinary school. "Oh, wow. Look at this." Tess pointed, and Janice moved behind her to where she could easily read the screen. "She graduated from Cleveland Culinary Institute. Do you have any idea how much money it costs to go to a school like that? A year's salary, pretty much. Well, teacher's salary, anyway. It's a risky venture to go to culinary school, and it doesn't always pay off. Not everyone has a great job waiting for them in a five-star restaurant when they graduate."

"Sandie has to have money from someplace," Janice said. "She just opened her own shop, after all. See what else you can find on her."

Tess did a bit more searching and landed on an article from a Cleveland newspaper dated a few years back. Tess released her hands from the keyboard and leaned back in the chair.

"Oh, wow." She quoted directly from the article: "'Dean and Julia Ballard passed away after a tragic car accident while en route to a local charity event. They leave behind one daughter, Sandie. Dean Ballard gained notoriety earlier this year when his law firm won a large class-action suit against Cleveland pharmaceutical company Stalwart Alliance.'"

"Wow." Janice leaned over to have a closer look. "So Sandie lost both of her parents at the same time. I can't even imagine. And she must have been really young at the time. If she was the only surviving child, as this article says, then maybe she used inheritance monies to pay for school. That's a thought."

"And to invest in her new bakery." Tess crossed her arms. "I'm going to shut this down now. I feel like a snoop."

Janice felt bad as well, somehow, suspecting Sandie Ballard. Maybe the young woman was simply trying to make it in a new town. Maybe she'd come to visit with Georgia to... Well, Janice couldn't think of a logical reason, but surely there was one.

Janice left the office and helped Robin tidy up the café. Then she headed back into the kitchen just in time to see Winnie opening the oven door for a peek inside.

Winnie closed the door and fanned herself with her hand. "I just wish it wasn't so hot in here. There's nothing worse than baking in August. What's wrong with that AC, anyway?"

"Nothing that I know of," Janice responded. "The rest of the inn is cool enough. In fact, it doesn't feel particularly warm in here either. At least not to me."

"Really?" Winnie fanned herself. "Feels like an oven to me."

"Maybe you're just stressed from working so hard," Georgia said. "You'll get overheated. It's not safe or healthy."

"Oh, I'll be fine." Winnie waved a dishrag in the air. "I'm resilient."

Janice couldn't help but agree. Winnie always seemed to pull through, no matter what she faced.

Or, maybe she didn't.

Janice sniffed at the air, noticing a scorched smell. "Smells like something's burning."

"Oh, for the love of Pete!" Winnie wiped her hands on her apron, then sprinted toward the stove. She lifted the lid on the kettle, and the odor grew stronger. "Did I really just scorch the potatoes?"

"Smells like it." Georgia reached for the pot and moved it to another burner, one that was turned off. "Don't fret, Winnie. I'm sure it's just the ones on bottom that are burnt." She coughed as a puff of acrid steam rose from the kettle. "I'll pull out the ones on top and add extra butter and cream. We probably cooked too many anyway. It'll be fine."

A familiar voice sounded from the lobby. "Yoo-hoo! Is anyone here? I've got exciting news that involves Winnie!"

Janice recognized Margaret Ashworth's voice at once.

"Want me to tell her you're too busy, Winnie?" Janice asked.

Winnie groaned and set the pan of mashed potatoes aside. "No, I'll go out there. Just give me a bit to get my composure."

In a few minutes Janice and Winnie headed to the lobby to meet with Margaret, leaving Georgia in charge of the kitchen.

As they approached, Janice couldn't help but notice Margaret's wrinkled nose.

"Is something burning? The oddest smell is coming from the kitchen."

"Nothing to worry about," Winnie countered as she straightened her apron. "What's your news, Margaret?"

The petite woman grinned and clasped her hands together. "To celebrate your victory, Winnie, we're doing a special baking-themed exhibit at the museum until the end of August. I've gathered other historians from this area who have been researching baking techniques during the 1850s. We're going to have the most exciting exhibit ever."

Winnie's brown eyes widened. "Oh my, that sounds wonderful."

"I'm so excited I could just bust a gut. We've got three period stoves coming in, along with several recipe books that date back to the 1700s. But here's where it gets really exciting. On Thursday the fifteenth—that's one week from today—we want to have an interactive portion where we feature a real baker, serving up bread just as they would have done in the 1850s."

"Sounds like a lot of work," Janice said doubtfully. "And it's just two days before the state competition."

Winnie's eyes were shining. "Yes, but think of the publicity for the inn."

"Right." Margaret paused. "And, of course, we want to feature you at the exhibit, Winnie. But we realize your schedule is crazy right now, so we've also asked Sandie Ballard to bake for us that day. She was happy to oblige. In fact, she was downright giddy. She's new in town and hasn't met a lot of people yet, so she felt this would be a good way to introduce herself."

Winnie's smile faded. "But I, well…"

"You wouldn't believe how excited Sandie is to share the experience with you. My goodness, but she sang your praises. I think you've got a real fan there. So, what do you say? Would it be asking too much for you to come for a couple of hours? We'll start the interactive portion promptly at noon."

"Oh, well, I…" Winnie's words drifted off. "I forgot about the café there for a minute."

Janice couldn't stand to see her look so disappointed. "We can do the meal prep in advance for that day, and Robin can take charge." She patted Winnie's arm. "I bet many of our regulars would come to the exhibit anyway."

"Please say yes!" Margaret seemed elated at the prospect. "We made a lovely sign, singing your praises as Marietta's Rising Star. And I thought it would be very appropriate if you could say a few words before the event, welcome the crowd, maybe give them a few bread baking tips, and then pass them off to Sandie, who will demonstrate the ovens."

A hint of a smile passed over Winnie's face. "I think I could do that. And thank you for the kindness."

"Are you kidding me? You're the one doing us the favor. If I tell the people of Marietta that our own rising star will be there in person, they'll flock to the event. We'll have a line halfway down the block."

"I doubt that." Winnie did not look convinced.

"Well, Sandie will sing your praises. She's a nervous wreck, but I know that being in your presence will calm her. You have that effect on people, Winnie."

A hint of a smile reappeared on Winnie's face. "I really need to take the time to get to know her, sounds like. I'm guessing we have a lot in common."

Winnie agreed to be at the event, but Janice secretly wondered if her friend was up to it. With so much on her proverbial plate, Winnie was already exhausted. Still, if she wanted to add one more thing to her to-do list, who was Janice to stop her?

CHAPTER TWELVE

Janice spent the rest of that day fretting over Winnie, who worked tirelessly in the kitchen on her pie recipes. She even stayed late that afternoon, something that rarely happened. Winnie and Georgia finally left around six and arrived extra early on Friday morning.

By the time the guests were coming down for breakfast, Janice was really getting worried when the expected cinnamon rolls were nowhere to be found. She made a quick dash into the kitchen in search of them.

"Winnie, we promised Reena some of your cinnamon rolls, but I can't find them for some reason. Where did you hide them?"

"Hmm?" Winnie turned, and Janice noticed the distracted look on her face and dark circles under her eyes. "I hid something?"

"Just asking where the cinnamon rolls are. They're on the menu board for today, but I can't find them. Did you hide them away from Robin and Taylor? I know they've been partial to your sweets of late."

"Hey, don't blame me!" Robin entered the room and reached for a coffee cup. "I didn't steal any."

"They're on the countertop, right where they always are." Winnie gestured with her hand and then got back to work on her blueberry pie.

Janice looked around but couldn't see any rolls. Surely Georgia had just moved them to a different spot to make room for all of the goings-on in the kitchen. Janice continued to search—every counter, the pantry, even the top of the fridge. There were no cinnamon rolls to be found. Either they had a Houdini in their midst, or Winnie had forgotten to bake them.

She pulled Georgia aside. "Do you have any idea where I can find the cinnamon rolls? Winnie's so distracted, I think she forgot where she put them. I've looked everywhere I can think of."

Georgia shook her head. "She didn't make any cinnamon rolls this morning."

"What? Are you sure?"

"I thought it was strange too. She told me last night she would be coming in extra early to make them because she was too tired yesterday afternoon. But when we got here this morning, I figured she changed her mind because she didn't start the recipe. In fact, all she could talk about was pies. I was afraid to ask about the cinnamon rolls because she seems so out-of-sorts. Did you notice?"

"Yes. It's just so strange. She told me that they were in the same place as usual. How could she completely forget to make them and then forget she forgot?"

Janice walked out to the café and made apologies to Reena, who opted for a cranberry-orange scone. About midmorning, after the café closed till lunch, she headed to the office to have a chat with Tess.

After hearing the news, Tess seemed as perplexed as Janice. "That's so strange. It's not like Winnie to forget anything. Maybe she really did make them, and Georgia just didn't see them."

"No, she really forgot. I can tell you the kitchen doesn't smell like cinnamon and sugar this morning. I always love that smell when the cinnamon rolls are in the oven." Janice couldn't imagine how stressed Winnie must be to forget her signature cinnamon rolls. "I think we're all going a little crazy lately. Things have been a bit chaotic."

"Let's get LuAnn and take a walk so we can talk about it without anyone overhearing." A few minutes later they left the inn in the care of Robin and Taylor and set off together under clear skies.

"Let's head over to the Sassy Seamstress," Tess suggested. "They're having a sale."

The three friends strolled down the sidewalk in the direction of the fabric shop. The heat, coupled with the high humidity, was nearly more than Janice could handle. As they rounded a turn in the road, the river came into view.

Janice stared out over the waters of the Ohio at the very point where it met the Muskingum, and she watched in wonder as the two became one. She couldn't help but think about how the rivers kept moving, in spite of any obstacles. She knew what that felt like. She'd faced days—more than she could count— where getting out of bed in the morning, putting one foot in front of the other—felt impossible. Like there was a dam holding back the river's flow. But somehow, with God's help, she'd pushed through not just the loss of Lawrence, but an empty nest too. Now, bravely facing this new chapter of her life, she could look at that river and feel its current once again. What she felt energized her, brought excitement she hadn't felt in some time.

"You okay over there, Janice?" Tess slipped her arm through the crook of Janice's and smiled. "You're suspiciously quiet."

"Just reflective," Janice said. "And hot."

"Me too." LuAnn fanned herself with her hand. "I'm half-tempted to jump in that river just to cool down."

"Nah, you don't want to have to fix your hair all over again," Janice said. "Let's just keep moving. Maybe we'll catch a breeze."

Janice was grateful when they finally reached the store. One step inside, and the AC made everything right again. After cooling down, they *oohed* and *aahed* over every lovely bolt of fabric. Janice loved the selections of bright summery patterns. She pulled out a bolt of cotton in the prettiest shades of pink and green and examined it with a critical eye. "This reminds me of Sandie Ballard, all of that pink and lime green. Seems to be trendy right now, I guess."

"I guess." Tess shrugged. "Not really my speed though."

They were interrupted by a cheery greeting from the shop owner, Wendy Wilson. "Welcome to the Sassy Seamstress."

"Thanks, Wendy." Janice held up a bolt of teal cotton. "Do you think this color looks good with my skin tone? I'm awfully pale for such bright colors."

From the other side of the bolts, LuAnn laughed. "Hey, if Reena Newberry can get away with it, you can. I've never seen anyone with skin that pale."

"True," Janice said.

"I agree, you could wear that color easily." Wendy beckoned to her. "But if you're partial to teals, come up to the front of the store with me. I've got a bolt of cotton print similar to this with slightly less than a yard left on it. I'm letting it go for half price. Want to take a look?"

"Sure, sounds great."

Janice followed behind Wendy, who led her to a bolt near the front of the store. Though she didn't know when she might find time to sew, Janice agreed to take the colorful fabric. As Wendy rang her up, she lowered her voice to have a quiet conversation with Janice and the others.

"While you're here, ladies, I have a question for you."

"Sure. What's up?" Tess asked.

"Well..." Wendy paused and looked around, as if worried about someone overhearing. "First of all, I read Hank Clive's most recent article on Winnie. He went way overboard in the way he portrayed the inn. I was shocked."

"Agreed," Janice said. "I've given thought to contacting the editor-in-chief, but I don't know that it would do much good now. I do think an apology or retraction is in order though."

"That's why I haven't said anything until now. I don't want to hurt Winnie any more than she's already hurt. But as you know, I was one of the bread recipients."

"Oh dear." Tess shook her head. "What did your note say?"

Wendy leaned forward and spoke in hushed tones. "Cancel your reservation, or face the consequences."

"Ugh." Janice, LuAnn, and Tess groaned simultaneously.

"It was on a little pink paper," Wendy explained. "Laminated. I still can't figure out if it was baked into the loaf or inserted after the fact. If it was baked in, I can't figure out why it didn't melt."

"We don't know the answer to that ourselves." Janice tucked the bag of fabric under her arm. "But we're going to keep looking into it until we figure it out."

Wendy handed her a receipt. "For a minute, I pondered the notion that Margaret at the historical society had done this to stir up interest in her upcoming baking exhibit. I know the display has something to do with bread, right?"

"Yes. She's invited Winnie and Sandie Ballard to come and bake loaves of bread in an antique oven next Thursday, just two days before the Rising Star finals in Columbus."

"I can't believe Winnie has time for all that."

"She doesn't." Janice shifted the bag of fabric to her other arm. "She's drowning in work. Thank goodness she's done baking extra loaves of bread now, and I don't think anyone found messages in the second batch she made—which is great news. But we're trying to get her to slow down. She's doing entirely too much. I'm really worried about her."

"I saw her at the grocery store the other day, and she looked absolutely exhausted. I tried to tell her that no contest is worth it." Wendy clucked her tongue. "But I could tell my words were going in one ear and out the other. You know how she is, always looking after the interests of others first."

Yes, Janice knew, all right.

The ladies thanked Wendy and headed back out onto the sidewalk. In spite of the heat, they paused to chat.

"I hate to hear that," Janice said. "Every day another bread recipient reports in."

"I could kick myself for suggesting those free loaves of bread," LuAnn said. "Winnie's plate was full, even before all of this. What was I thinking?"

"You were thinking we could ride the wave, and she would have a great time, that's what you were thinking. And she has enjoyed this," Janice said.

"Up to a point," Tess said. "But exhaustion is setting in."

"I agree." LuAnn looked troubled by this conversation. "I feel like we're taking advantage of her."

"At least she has Georgia." Tess sighed. "I think she's letting Georgia help her some, but we all know Winnie would rather do everything herself."

LuAnn shrugged. "You know how it is. She's ten times better at everything in the kitchen than any of us. It's hard to compete."

Janice thought that through and wondered if they hadn't all come to that same conclusion. "True, but this was never about a competition, at least not between us."

Tess shrugged. "I know, but you know when you're in the presence of greatness. Winnie Washington is…well, great.

And sometimes I walk out of the kitchen feeling like I was silly to walk in in the first place."

Janice shook her head. "We own that kitchen, Tess. You should feel right at home, no matter who else is in there. That was our plan—one for all and all for one."

"Right." Tess nodded. "I haven't forgotten. And I'm perfectly happy to help out, but when it comes to the cooking, the real cooking, I feel like we need to let our light shine—and Winnie is our brightest light."

"I guess that's true. I just don't want our shiniest bulb to crash and burn because we didn't lend enough support." Janice was struck with a fabulous idea. "Hey, I know! When this event is behind us, let's send her off on a vacation."

LuAnn nodded. "Fantastic idea! Now, let's keep moving before I melt into the sidewalk."

They left the store and ran into Brad Grimes leaving his realty office.

"Hey, Brad." LuAnn offered him a broad smile. "Closing down shop in the middle of the day?"

"Only for an hour or so. Remember, I told you Winnie invited me over to sample some new pie recipe. She says I have the best palate in town."

"She said you were her official taste tester." LuAnn grinned. "And yes, she's baking today, same as pretty much every day. I think the flavor of the day is blueberry. Or maybe she said Bob Andy? Is that a thing?"

"Yes." Janice chimed in. "Bob Andy is a pie. Custard, with cinnamon and cloves. I think it's an Amish thing."

"I like cinnamon." Brad licked his lips. "But, honestly? If she keeps inviting me over for taste tests, I'm going to have to move my belt buckle over a notch. The other day I sampled her key lime. After that came buttermilk pie." He pooched his stomach and gave it a rub, then laughed. "Not sure how much more of this I can take, especially with this new bakery going in so close to my office. I'm going to need to keep an eye on my blood sugar if I can't get things under control. And don't even get me started on Thelma and Irene. I've been taking sweets to their place for days now. Neither of those ladies needs all that sugar, but they keep thinking of new things they want to try."

"I know exactly how you and your aunts feel." LuAnn chuckled. "That's one reason we're out for a walk today, to burn off the calories."

"How are things going on your end?" Brad looked back and forth between them. "Any clues as to who might have sabotaged the bread?"

"The field is wide open," Janice said. "But we can't pinpoint anyone or anything. Georgia has been acting odd."

"How so?"

"She seems a bit secretive."

"And one of our guests, Reena Newberry, is a bit suspicious too," LuAnn added.

Janice felt beads of sweat trickle down her back. "Yes, we caught her sneaking into the kitchen in the wee hours of the night."

"The night the bread was baked?" Brad asked.

"No." Janice shook her head. "The night after they had all been handed out. But hearing the noise reminded me that Huck barked on Monday night too."

"Could've been the wind." He shrugged.

LuAnn frowned. "We've got our feelers out for Hank Clive."

"Hank? What's he done?"

"Like Georgia and Reena, he was there on the day Winnie was baking. He kept trying to come into the kitchen."

"But that makes sense, if he was doing a story on Winnie," Brad countered.

"That's what he *said* he was doing," Tess responded.

Brad did not look convinced. "I don't see that he has motive. Why would he have it out for Wayfarers Inn? You've never done anything to him."

"No, but he does love a good story. Did you see the article about Winnie in yesterday's paper?"

Brad nodded. "I confess, I did. I was surprised. I thought he speculated a little too much."

"A little?" All three women spoke at once.

"Okay, a lot."

Tess sighed. "We're no closer to finding out who did this than we were a few days back, but we're not giving up."

"I called Randy Lewis this morning," Brad said. "Just wanted to give him a heads-up so he's aware."

"I'm glad it was you and not one of us." Janice shifted the bag of fabric to her other arm, now feeling the heat more than ever. "Winnie didn't want us to involve the police. I think she was afraid it would bring bad publicity to the inn."

"They're keeping an eye out for anyone or anything that looks suspicious." Brad glanced at his watch. "Oh, sorry. I've got to run. After meeting with Winnie, I've got an appointment."

"See you later, Brad," LuAnn said.

"And by the way, tell those aunts of yours that we said hello," Tess added. "Things have been so busy that we've scarcely had time for a visit."

"Will do." Brad flashed a bright smile, then said his good-byes—with a special smile for LuAnn—and headed off toward the inn.

CHAPTER THIRTEEN

The ladies found themselves in front of the new bakery, where they stopped to have a closer look.

"You've got to admit, that's a cute name," LuAnn said as she examined the sign above the shop. "The Better Batter."

Tess shrugged. "A little too cutesy for me, but then, what do I know?"

"I know I like cupcakes," Janice said, "And she's advertising a salted caramel cupcake with a free cup of coffee."

LuAnn grinned. "I could never turn down a free cup of coffee."

"Of course not." Janice feigned innocence. "We need to size up the competition, right?"

"I wouldn't say she's competition," LuAnn countered. "We don't own a bakery. We just happen to have the best baker in town at our inn, that's all."

"Not according to that sign." Janice pointed up again and gave Tess a pleading look. "Come with us. All for one, remember? Besides, you need to save me from myself. I cannot be held responsible for what I might purchase in a bakery after walking in this heat."

"After all we've eaten over the past few days?" Tess argued. "Are you kidding? Whatever happened to burning off calories?"

She waved dismissively. "I don't think I can handle any more sweets, thank you very much."

Still, Janice and LuAnn managed to coax her inside. Janice could hardly believe her eyes—or her nose—when they entered the colorful shop. The décor was delightful, in varying shades of pink and lime green. But what really grabbed her attention were the glass cases filled with every kind of baked good one could ever dream of—cookies with sprinkles, colorful cupcakes, adorably decorated cake balls, tiered cakes, and breads. Lots and lots of breads.

"Oh, wow." Janice paused to take it all in and turned her attention to a familiar young woman from the church youth group. Janice smiled and waved. "Hi, Jennie!"

Jennie reciprocated the wave and headed their way, face lit in a smile. "Glad to see you all. If you're hungry, we're having a special on cupcakes today. Lots of different flavors available, but our special of the day is salted caramel."

Before they could respond, Sandie Ballard emerged from the kitchen. She had a cell phone pressed to her ear. She was giving someone on the other end of the line a real earful. As she listened, Janice realized that Sandie's irritated demeanor didn't match the cute, sweet setting of the shop.

Sandie continued to rail at the person on the other end of the line, then ended the call with a "Humph!" Afterward she muttered something that Janice had to strain to make out: "Telling me I got it wrong."

Interesting.

Sandie turned to face Janice and the others and offered what appeared to be a forced smile. "Sorry about that. What can I do for you folks?" Her words lacked the enthusiasm one would expect from a new business owner.

"We wanted to come and see the place," Tess explained.

"Speak for yourself." Janice laughed and walked over to the glass cases. "I'm here for a cupcake."

"They're very good." Jennie's eyes sparkled as she gestured to the glass cases. "My favorite is the mocha cream."

"Mmm, that sounds delicious. What else do you recommend?"

"Well, since you asked, we've got a wide variety of selections, including cookie butter, birthday cake, lemon raspberry, key lime, and more." Sandie's personality switched immediately, and she transformed into a bubbly, effervescent shop owner right in front of them. "I know who you ladies are. I've been wanting to meet the rest of you after meeting Janice at the competition."

Jennie sprang into action, making introductions. "Sandie, meet Tess and LuAnn. They and Janice own Wayfarers Inn."

Sandie shook their hands. "So, what's your pleasure today, ladies?"

Before the others could argue, Janice ordered a dozen cupcakes to go—in pretty much every flavor Sandie offered.

As Sandie filled their box, she chatted with them—all flattering comments about Winnie's big win at the contest. "I'm so tickled you've come to see me, though I'm awfully surprised, what with the town's best baker working in your own kitchen." She giggled nervously. "Better not tell her you stopped by here."

"We won't, trust me." Janice stared at the box of colorful cupcakes. "I guess we'll have to eat the evidence before we get back."

"Speak for yourself." LuAnn shook her head. "I'm not eating a dozen cupcakes. Not in one sitting, anyway."

"Take a few by Brad's office next door." Sandie's lips curled up in a smile. "He's a real sweetie, and he's fallen in love with my mocha cream."

"He did mention it to me," said LuAnn, smiling at Sandie.

"Yes, he's in every morning buying scones or muffins or a slice of my chocolate chip banana bread. And he loves my coffee." She pointed at the board advertising her specials. "Could I interest you in a cup? Hazelnut."

"Sounds delicious," LuAnn said. "Yes, please."

After paying for their cupcakes and thanking Sandie for their coffee, the friends walked out with their to-go cups and LuAnn carrying the cupcake box.

"On second thought, I'm not too sure about this." Tess plopped down onto the bench outside the bakery. "Do you think with the stress Winnie's been under that she'll appreciate us buying someone else's cupcakes?"

"Don't worry," Janice said. "She'll never see them."

"I hope you're not saying we're going to eat them all right now." LuAnn looked floored by this notion.

"Before we get back to the inn? Probably not." Janice grinned. "I say we have a tasting party to see what flavors we like. I'm starting with the key lime."

"I guess I could have just one." Tess stuck her hand in the box that Janice held and came out with red velvet. "But don't you dare tell my waistline."

"Hmm." LuAnn stared down at the assortment. "I'll go with the cookies and cream. It won't hurt to take a tiny bite."

Janice took a bite of her cupcake. Goodness gracious goat, this was good. She took another little bite, then the ladies passed around all three of their cupcakes so everyone could have sample bites.

"I have to admit, it's really hard to resist." LuAnn wiped some frosting from her lips. "But we really should slow down."

"Yes, it was good, to say the least." Janice paused and pondered a second cupcake.

"The cupcake was a lot sweeter than their baker was when we first arrived," Tess observed.

Janice turned to face her friend. "You caught that too?"

Tess nodded. "I thought she was a bit...testy when she first came into the room. She seemed okay after that, I guess."

"No kidding." Janice brushed crumbs from her fingers. "I wouldn't want to be on the other end of her temper."

LuAnn shrugged. "I guess everyone's entitled to a bad day every now and again. I've certainly had my share."

"Me too." Janice replayed the whole thing in her head once more. "You've got to give it to her, she's a hard worker. Did you notice all those other goodies? And what about all of those breads?" She wadded up her cupcake liner, tossed it into a nearby trash receptacle, and reached back into the box for another cupcake.

"I was too busy looking at all the cupcakes," Tess said. "Did they look good?"

"They sure did." Janice spoke around a bite of lemon-raspberry cupcake. "But her cinnamon rolls didn't look nearly as yummy as Winnie's." She nibbled on her cupcake and then licked her fingers. "Oh my stars, this is divine. But we can't go back with the box in hand. We're definitely going to have to hide the evidence to protect Winnie's feelings. I didn't think that all the way through before I ordered a whole box."

"I guess you're right." LuAnn shrugged.

"No point in stirring that pot," Tess agreed.

"Better if we don't mention it at all," Janice said. "Mum's the word." She chuckled. "Or maybe I should say 'Mmm's' the word!" She took another bite of her cupcake, suddenly feeling a bit nauseous. She closed the lid on the cupcake box. "Just saying, we're going to have to figure out what to do with the rest of these once we get back to the inn. I think I'll text Robin and ask her to meet me in the lobby. I'll pass them off to her, and she can share them with Taylor."

"And you think Winnie won't figure it out?" Tess gave her a skeptical look.

"Maybe not. She's so busy, you know."

The front door of Sandie's shop opened, and she bolted out. Her knitted brow and down-turned lips were all the clues Janice needed to know that something was terribly wrong with this young woman.

Without even acknowledging them, Sandie took off down the sidewalk toward town.

"She's going someplace in a hurry," Janice observed.

"If she's headed to Brad's office, he's not there. I guess we were right in assuming she's having a bad day." Tess stared after Sandie, who clipped her way down the sidewalk with a scowl on her face. "Either that, or the building's on fire, and she's running to get away from it."

"No telling." Janice squinted as Sandie rounded a corner and disappeared from view. "But my antenna is up where she's concerned. There's something strange about that woman."

"Do you think she's bitter over losing the contest?" Tess asked.

Janice paused to think that through before responding. "I don't know why she would be. She came in second place, after all."

"That's an admirable thing, to come in second." LuAnn rose and tossed her empty cupcake liner into the trash can, then licked her fingertips clean.

Tess quirked a brow. "Try telling that to a silver medalist at the Olympics. A silver medalist is the top loser, if you think about it."

"Well, I never thought about it before," Janice said. "But I guess that's true."

Tess nodded. "Yep. Of all the losers in the Rising Star competition, Sandie was on top. And judging from the sour look on her face when she saw us in her shop, I can't help but wonder if it's bothering her. Maybe we'd better stop calling her shop the Better Batter and switch it to the *bitter* batter."

"Speak for yourself." LuAnn brushed her hands on her slacks. "She's really winning me over with these flavors."

"Just saying she's probably a little upset over not winning the contest, that's all. I would be."

"She's runner-up. If anything happens to Winnie, she'll be first in line—" Janice stopped short of saying "to compete at the finals." For the first time it occurred to her that Sandie actually had something to gain from Winnie's misfortune with the bread. Was she really, as Tess suggested, bitter? If so, had she somehow coerced Georgia into helping her sabotage their good friend?

CHAPTER FOURTEEN

On Saturday morning, a couple of Wayfarers guests checked out, and several more checked in. Reena Newberry was still firmly ensconced in Sunshine and Daisies. Janice headed into the office midmorning to take care of some paperwork and was joined by LuAnn.

"Do you have a minute?" Janice asked her.

"Sure." LuAnn leaned against the doorframe. "What's up? You look a little down in the dumps this morning."

Janice gestured for LuAnn to join her in the office for a private conversation. "I am a little concerned," Janice said. "Take a look at our reservation calendar." She pointed to the calendar on the computer screen.

"What about it?" LuAnn asked.

"We've had three more cancellations."

With the wave of a hand LuAnn appeared to dismiss the idea. "That's nothing to worry about, Janice. You know that. Things will pick back up again. It's the end of summer, after all. People are focused on getting their kids ready to go back to school."

"I'm just wondering if those notes are really scaring people off. Weren't we just turning away guests because there was no room at the inn? Now we can barely get them in the door."

"That's a bit of an exaggeration, don't you think?" LuAnn scratched her head. "Did anyone mention the notes?"

"No, but their reasons were really vague. One canceled because of a change of plans. Another because she just decided she couldn't afford time away from her work."

"And the third?" LuAnn asked.

"He didn't give a reason. Just called to cancel. And I wasn't brave enough to ask."

"I'm glad you didn't ask. I think it's better to say nothing at this point. But, man, I hope this doesn't keep up."

"It's my fault." Winnie's voice sounded from the office door.

Janice was mortified that Winnie had overheard the conversation, but there was no backpeddling now. The best she could do was offer encouragement where she could. "No, it most certainly is not, Winnie. You didn't put those notes in the bread."

Winnie leaned against the doorjamb. "Right, but I must've somehow left the loaves vulnerable to attack."

"That's just silly," LuAnn countered. "What baker ever had to guard the merchandise so someone wouldn't sabotage it?"

"This baker." Winnie raised her hand. "I've thought it through from a dozen different directions and still can't figure out how it happened. Yes, I left the dough alone while proofing, so I suppose someone could've slipped in and put the notes into the dough then. And, of course, I left the loaves sitting to cool. As sharp at that laminate was, I suppose the notes could've been poked in after baking. But I didn't notice any odd marks on the bread. Then again, there was so much going on the day I baked that first round. Folks in and out. The nosy reporter. A new guest. Stuff like that."

"I say we put it out of our minds and forge ahead," LuAnn said. "We're all firm believers in prayer. Let's all agree to pray that the Lord will turn this situation around in His timing and shine His light on the truth."

Winnie and Janice both agreed to do that. In fact, Janice had already been praying over the situation for days now.

Apparently, Winnie had too. She reached over and put her hand on Janice's arm. "Speaking of turning things over to the Lord, I wanted to tell you that I read a scripture today and saw it as if for the first time."

"Which one, Winnie?" Janice asked.

"It's the story of Pilate handing Barabbas over to the people. I guess I'd never realized it before, but Pilate did that because of public outcry. The people wanted Barabbas, they didn't want Jesus. It just hit me so hard—if Pilate hadn't been so hung up on satisfying the crowd, the whole of history might've been changed."

"Oh, I see." Janice paused to think it through.

"Now, I know that Pilate's actions were all part of a greater plan. I know that Jesus came to die, and if Pilate hadn't turned on Him, someone else would have. But today this scripture really got me to thinking about how many times I bow to peer pressure for the same reason Pilate did—wanting to satisfy the crowd." She paused as tears brimmed her lashes. "I know it's silly, but I want people to like what I do. I want to make them happy. I think that's why this whole thing is hitting me so hard."

"Oh, Winnie, we all do that," Janice said. "Trust me, as a pastor's wife I was such a people pleaser. I wanted folks to love me."

Winnie wiped her eyes. "I certainly never thought I'd relate to Pilate, but maybe I'm more like him than I thought. And I know I'm not alone. I'm a lover, not a hater. I want to be loved in return. It's unfathomable to me that people might think I would deliberately do something to hurt the inn or any of you."

"No one who truly knows you would believe that, Winnie. Everyone knows you've been set up. We've been set up."

"I guess I spend too much time worrying about what 'they' think. I wonder if my need for love and acceptance isn't too strong, too important."

After a group hug, Winnie headed off to the grocery store. Janice and LuAnn were just wrapping up in the office when Tess came in. "This is all so confusing," she said. "I've been going back through that day, over and over again."

"Which day?" Janice asked.

"The day Winnie baked the dozen loaves of bread."

"We had quite a few people coming and going from the inn just after she won that competition, so I didn't pay much attention to anyone in particular."

"Me neither," Tess admitted. "It could have been anyone— guests, well-wishers, folks coming to make reservations for the fall."

"Speaking of which…" Janice closed the door and pointed to the computer screen. "I was just telling LuAnn that more people are canceling their discount reservations since the notes in the bread incidents. I'm past the point where I can say it's just a coincidence. We've really been hard hit by this prank, if that's what it is. The people who are canceling are giving excuses, but I'm sure those in town who've discovered the notes have called their friends and relatives and told them to cancel."

"I still can't figure out who would have reason to want to hurt us—or to hurt Winnie." Tess sighed. "At least Reena hasn't been scared off."

"Speaking of Reena, did you hear her up walking the floors again last night?" Tess's voice grew more animated.

"No, I was exhausted," LuAnn said. "Fell asleep right away, in fact."

"Me too," Janice said.

"Well, I didn't." Tess began to pace the small office. "I couldn't sleep for some reason. Something was niggling at the back of my mind about Prudence's diary, so I went down to the office to get it. As I was coming down the stairs, I heard the elevator running. Sure enough, it was Reena again." She arched her eyebrows at the others, obviously expecting a reaction.

LuAnn didn't disappoint. "Did she go into the kitchen and swipe cookies again?"

Tess sighed. "No. She said hi to me and then went to the café and got a couple of snickerdoodles from the basket Winnie had left. I waited for her, and we walked back up the stairs together."

"Yep, she does love her snickerdoodles." Janice laughed. "Maybe she's getting ready for the apocalypse by stocking up on Winnie's sweets."

This got a laugh out of LuAnn. "I wish I knew what she was up to. There's got to be something else going on."

Tess leaned against the wall and crossed her arms over her chest. A smile tipped up the edges of her lips. "I did something on the sly."

Janice looked her way, more perplexed than ever. "What's that?"

"Come see for yourselves," said Tess.

CHAPTER FIFTEEN

August 4, 1860

Jason, of course, saw them coming long before they reached the house. The front door flew open, and he came rushing out and down the road to them. He took the bulk of William's weight from Prudence's arm, asking no questions until they reached the safety and privacy behind their closed door.

Prudence explained all to him in hurried whispers as she prepared supper. William was resting with a cup of coffee at the table, and Jason had retrieved Moses from the bedroom where he'd awakened from his nap. Their son had been walking for a few months now, and he happily toddled over to William, showing him the wooden horse Jason had made for his first birthday earlier that summer.

Prudence invited Jason to join William at the table, where she dished up bowls of soup for both men and herself. So many questions ran through her mind, but she would wait until they'd eaten a few bites before diving in. As it happened, William was the one who broke the silence.

"I know I scared thee back at the inn, Prudence. I did not mean to do that, and I am sorry."

"No harm done. But help me understand. Why is thee here? Is thee headed north?"

"Yes, I am." He took another bite. "I am headed to Pittsburgh at first light." He put his spoon down and dug in his waistcoat pocket, eventually bringing out a piece of folded paper. He eased the flaps open, and a gold ring—a small, perfect band—fell out onto the table.

Prudence gasped. "Oh, William." She'd never seen anything so perfect—or so valuable—in all her life.

He glanced her way and then pressed the ring into her hands. "This is why I am traveling to Pittsburgh with all haste."

Prudence held it in the palm of her hand. "A ring?"

William took a deep breath. "I have a friend back in Lexington. His name is Theodore. Our families live on neighboring farms. About ten years ago, my uncle and his family from Pittsburgh started to spend the summers visiting us. My young cousin, Birdie—let's see, she would have been about seven years old that first summer—attached herself to Theodore and me. At first we dismissed her. We were nine-year-old boys, after all, and sure we could outrun, outclimb, and outfish her. But Birdie wasn't so easily dismissed, and before many days had passed, we were, all three of us, best of friends."

He stopped speaking, and his eyes grew pensive. Then he shook his head, as if bringing himself back to the story. "Every summer was the same...until it was not. I don't know when it happened, maybe when Theodore turned sixteen and Birdie was thirteen. It was still the three of us, inseparable. But a gradual shift was happening, Theodore and Birdie's friendship was becoming something deeper, and we all felt it."

Prudence smiled. Well she remembered her feelings for Jason when she was fifteen and he was a few years older.

William continued. "A month ago, on her eighteenth birthday, Theodore asked Birdie to marry him. I have never seen a man so beside himself with joy as Theodore was when she said yes." William sighed. "But her father forbade it, saying there was a man back in Pittsburgh he meant for her to marry. Theodore was devastated. But he is not one to give up easily. He believes that she will refuse to marry this other man and will wait for him to come to her if he sends that ring to let her know his intentions."

Jason looked puzzled. "But why must thee take the ring? Why does Theodore not take it to her himself?"

William looked down at his hands. "Theodore's father passed away last year, and his mother is gravely ill. He cannot leave her. He has younger siblings who depend on him and need him at this time. It is his duty to stay with them."

"And thee has offered to go for him?" Prudence couldn't keep the incredulity from her voice.

"He is my friend—we are closer than brothers," William said simply. "We have grown up from our infancy together. I would travel much farther than this for his happiness. As he would for mine."

"David and Jonathan," Prudence said softly. She stood to clear the table.

"It is fortunate," said Jason, "that the thief that accosted thee did not find that ring."

William touched his temple gingerly. "Yes," he said. "I am trying to think of a way to better conceal it as I ride north."

Prudence froze, soup bowl in one hand, and the remaining loaf of bread in the other. "Oh," she said. "What if…"

William looked at her eagerly. "Thee has an idea?"

"What if I baked it into a loaf of bread?" Prudence said. "Thee could carry it in thy saddlebag to Pittsburgh, and no one would ever think there's something valuable in it."

For the second time since she'd met him, William's mouth dropped open in surprise.

Jason left to retrieve William's horse and, after helping William to a pallet in the corner, Prudence got busy making a loaf of bread. After she measured and stirred and kneaded the dough and left it to rise, she sat at the table, turning the ring in her fingers and pondering the love it represented. Not the love of a man for a woman—though it symbolized that too, of course—but the unselfish love of true friendship. She punched down the risen dough and shaped it into a loaf around the precious ring, leaving it to rise one more time before baking. It would be some time before she was able to lie down to sleep, but she didn't mind. It was her honor to do what she could for young love and true friendship.

CHAPTER SIXTEEN

Tess took a seat at the computer. She gestured for the ladies to look over her shoulder as she entered a web address.

"I did a little snooping into Reena Newberry's background last night," she admitted. "When I went back to my room I got on my laptop and started digging. And boy, oh boy, did I find some juicy material."

"Like what?" Janice asked.

"She's from Pennsylvania. Well-to-do family. From what I could gather, her parents were prominent in town. Grandparents too. I found a write-up in the paper about her great-great-grandmother, who had ties to the Civil War. I believe her name was Birdie. Hang on a second, and I'll try to pull it up." She scrolled through the site until she found what she wanted.

"What sort of ties?"

"Look here." Tess pointed at the computer screen. "According to this article, she lived for a summer in Lexington, Kentucky, with family members, then moved back to Pittsburgh, where her father forced her to marry one of the Newberrys."

"What do you mean, 'forced her to marry?'" Janice asked.

"Well, the article insinuates that she had planned to marry someone else, a young man from Lexington, but her father arranged for her to marry Edwin Newberry—I think that was his name, anyway—and she married him rather than being turned out of the house for defying her father." She scrolled to the article until she found what she was looking for. "Or Edwin might have won her over with his money. He was the richest guy in town."

"Huh." LuAnn seemed to be contemplating all of this. "So, she left behind fiancé number one to marry fiancé number two?"

Tess shrugged. "I couldn't find any more details. This article primarily focuses on their wedding. It was quite an elaborate affair. Listen to this." She read aloud from the article:

Our fair city was privy to the wedding of the decade last Saturday evening. Excitement spilled over from every guest who attended the nuptials of Birdie Atkinson and Edwin Newberry. It is rumored that many a neighbor took a peek through the bushes to see the bride and her faithful groom say their "I do's" on a beautiful April evening. Birdie, the oldest daughter of Henry and Maisie Atkinson, looked radiant in her elegant gown, which was fashioned out of pure white silk. The Brussels lace over-dress boasted a fitted bodice and full skirt. The bride held the guests enthralled with her lace veil, which was fashionably long and full. The entire event was a whirl and vortex of delight for all who were fortunate enough to attend.

"Wow. Sounds like quite the event," LuAnn said.

"Makes me wonder who the other fiancé was." Janice leaned forward to scan the article once again.

"Or if he could have competed with all of that," Tess added.

Janice shrugged. "I guess we'll never know." She couldn't help thinking about how sad it all sounded. What would it matter how lovely the event, if the bride did not love the groom?

"That's not all," Tess said. "I learned a lot more than just about her wedding. The Newberry family goes back generations. I got on an ancestry site and traced their lineage all the way back to Thomas Newberry, who arrived in America in 1630."

"My goodness." Janice was truly astounded by this news. "I don't know that any of us could trace our American roots back that far."

"Me neither. Thomas Newberry settled in Massachusetts. How they ended up in Pennsylvania, I'm not sure. But the family certainly has a rich heritage. And you should see the Newberry house." She started typing once again. "It's on the National Register of Historic Places and is one of the most frequently visited homes in Pittsburgh."

A few seconds later, a breathtaking view filled the screen.

"Whoa." Janice gazed in awe at the expansive house, which sat on the most magnificent grounds. The photo must have been taken in the fall, because the trees were chock-full of leaves in a variety of reds, golds, and oranges. But what really took her breath away was the house. "I've never seen anything like it."

"It got a big write-up in the Pittsburgh paper back in the mid-1800s." Tess read aloud from the article: "'The Newberry home boasts nine fireplaces and breathtaking original millwork. The house was constructed over two periods. The first stone house developed in 1782 and the second in the mid-1830s, when multiple bedrooms were added.'"

"How many bedrooms are we talking here?" LuAnn asked.

Tess skimmed the article. "Fifteen, each with their own full baths. It also has a ballroom and was considered to be the crown jewel of Pittsburgh, at least at the time of this article's writing."

LuAnn whistled. "Wow."

"The house, known to all as the cottage, has panoramic views." Tess clicked to a different website. "From what I can gather, the Newberry family still lives in the house today but opens it to the public on special occasions."

"I can't picture Reena Newberry opening her home to strangers, can you?" Janice couldn't even imagine the woman—who mostly kept to herself—swinging wide her doors for friends to enter.

"No way," Tess agreed. "But if I had a house like that, I'd show it off." She pointed at the screen. "The current appraisal on the house is over nine million dollars. I don't think I've ever seen anything that even comes close."

"I have." LuAnn leaned in to have a closer look. "Remember that old show with Robin Leach, *Lifestyles of the Rich and Famous?* They had lots of houses like this. Only, most were newer, and movie stars lived in them. New money, not old."

Janice was floored. To think that Reena Newberry lived in such a place was beyond her comprehension. "I certainly never thought I'd meet anyone who lived in a place like that, though. It's really magnificent."

"Right?" Tess scrolled to an interior view of the foyer. "It's been in the Newberry family for generations. Dates all the way back to Reena's great-great-great-grandfather. I'm not sure, though. I kind of lost track of the numbers before the greats. But I guess we can assume that Reena took back her Newberry name after her husband died."

"Or maybe she always kept it as part of her name," Janice suggested. "You know, like Catherine Zeta-Jones or Helena Bonham Carter."

"Could be." LuAnn shrugged. "I guess that would take a little more research."

"I'd rather look at more pictures of this amazing house." Tess scrolled through photos of the various rooms, and Janice let out a whistle when they got to the ornate dining room.

"You could host a dinner for forty at that table," she said. "Maybe more."

"Yes, and check out this master bedroom. If this is where Reena sleeps when she's at home, it's a wonder Sunshine and Daisies is good enough for her."

"This seems more like a country estate than a big-city home." Janice shook her head. "Makes me want to take a trip to Pittsburgh."

Tess shrugged. "Yep. Reena has traded in the most magnificent home I've ever seen for a tiny room at a B&B where she hides like a snickerdoodle-eating hermit."

"And won't let us clean up after her," LuAnn added. "I'm guessing she has all kinds of people on her staff at home."

"Very strange," Janice said as she took in the image of the house one last time. She couldn't make sense of it. The whole thing was very odd indeed.

Stranger still…Janice happened to catch a glimpse of the laminating machine in the corner of their office. Confusion registered at once as she observed that it was clean. Pristine. Dust free.

CHAPTER SEVENTEEN

The weekend passed quietly. On Monday morning, Janice entered the kitchen with a yawn. She managed a "Good morning" to Winnie, then walked over to the coffeepot and grabbed the handle with a grip so strong it would have landed an opponent on the floor of the ring. Thank the Lord for coffee, especially on days like today, when she'd spent half the night awake.

"You okay over there?" Winnie asked.

"Mm-hmm." Janice reached for a mug and filled it with the heavenly elixir, then took her first sip. Perfect. She leaned against the counter and closed her eyes. As she did, the scrumptious smell of breakfast casserole filled the air.

"You going back to sleep?" Winnie asked. "Kind of looks like it."

"Nope. Just thinking."

"Well, think over some food." Winnie opened the oven and reached for a mitt. She pulled out a casserole and set it on the stovetop, then scooped a big serving onto a plate and handed it to Janice.

"You don't need to wait on me, Winnie." Janice yawned and reached into the drawer for a fork.

"Looks like you're about to fall over."

"Mm-hmm." She jabbed her fork into the casserole and took her first bite. *Ouch.* Hot. But oh, so yummy.

"What's on your mind to keep you up all night?" Winnie asked as she turned back to her work seasoning some whole chickens.

Janice hated to share. She didn't want to make Winnie more anxious than she already was. But Janice had spent the last couple of nights thinking through everything she, Tess, and LuAnn had learned—both about Prudence and about Reena Newberry. Why had Reena come to Wayfarers? Certainly she had more on her agenda than sitting in her room day after day.

Janice had also spent quite a bit of time thinking through the situation with Georgia, who was acting more than a little strange of late. She seemed distracted when they were together. Something was definitely amiss there.

Janice noticed that Winnie was working alone this morning, so she asked the obvious question. "Where's Georgia?"

"She went out with Kip after church yesterday," Winnie responded. "He brought her back home around ten, but they were on the phone for hours after that. I could hear her from my room."

"They seem to be hitting it off."

"Yes, definitely. But I could tell she was worn out, so I told her to sleep in this morning. She deserves a break."

Janice had no problem offering Winnie a look of compassion as she responded, "So do you, Winnie."

"Maybe." Winnie shrugged. "But I've been more worried about Georgia. I've really been pushing that sweet girl to her limit. For someone who's not receiving a penny in salary, she works harder than anyone I know."

"True." Janice took another sip of her coffee and felt better at once. "But I know she's grateful to learn from you. She's getting a free education. You have to look at it that way."

"She's been a big help, that's for sure." Winnie transferred the chickens to a roasting pan. "With so much on my plate—pun intended—I've got to keep things rolling. She's really getting to know her way around the kitchen, and I'm glad about that."

"I know you're happy for the help. You've been working long and hard," Janice said. "Maybe it's time we gave you a vacation."

A comfortable smile tipped up the edges of Winnie's lips. "If I win the competition, I'll be happy to take a few days away. And don't forget, if I win, I'll get a trip on board the *Princess of the Seas* cruise ship where I'll learn from a master chef." She rubbed her hands together. "I don't know which excites me more—the part about the cruise, or working with a real master chef."

"*Pfft.* You don't need a master chef." Janice fought the temptation to roll her eyes. "You *are* a master chef."

"Don't be silly."

Winnie went back to work. Before long, she was mixing up dough for cinnamon rolls. Hopefully this time she would actually remember to bake and serve them. "Hope you'll excuse me," she said, "but I need to focus. I'm using a different recipe this time around."

Before long Winnie was humming a familiar hymn. Janice interrupted her. "Do you need any help, Winnie? I'm here for you, if so."

"Nope. I'm good." She went back to humming.

"Well, if you're sure." Janice stood watching for a moment, then decided her presence was probably more of a nuisance. She turned to walk out of the kitchen, but Winnie stopped her.

"You're not mad, are you?"

Janice turned back. "Mad? Why would I be mad?"

"Because I said I didn't need your help." Winnie looked up from her project and shrugged. "I wasn't trying to shoo you away. Sometimes I feel like I kind of blew in here and took over your kitchen. That wasn't my intention. Hope you know that."

"We're thrilled to have you."

"Good. Because I plan to stay put as long as you'll have me. And just for the record, I'm not the sort to retire. I want to go out, guns blazing."

"I think you mean Old Red's burners blazing."

"Same thing." Winnie chuckled.

"Just promise you'll take time to rest between cooking and baking sprees, Winnie. We'd like to keep you healthy and strong."

"I will, I promise. But just so we're clear, it's the competition that's getting to me, not my work here. I get my energy from my work, not from lounging around. That's just how I'm wired. Some of us are born workaholics, you know."

"I know. But even God took one day off." Janice winked at her friend. "Keep that in mind, will you? If the Almighty thought it was a worthy venture to put His feet up, maybe you should too."

"I will. Right after I finish these chickens. If I could just speak lunch into existence like God did with the stars and planets and such, I'd get finished a lot quicker."

Janice couldn't help but laugh at the image that presented. "I like the smell of your chickens in the oven, so I, for one, am glad these things take their time."

Just as they wrapped up their conversation, Tess and LuAnn entered the kitchen. Tess put a file folder down on the table, grabbed a cup, and filled it with coffee, LuAnn settled down at the table to read the paper, and Robin came in to empty the trash can. "Wait a minute!" Winnie put her hand up and pointed at the trash bag just as Robin reached for it. "What's up with all of these cupcake liners in the trash?" She pointed at the hot-pink papers. "I never use that color, so I know they aren't from my cupcakes."

"Oh, I, well..." Robin stumbled over her words, then looked at Winnie with a shrug. "I guess someone ate cupcakes?"

"From the new bakery, perhaps?" Winnie lifted the cupcake box from the trash and pointed to the logo featuring the Better Batter. "Robin, do you know anything about this?"

Robin stared at the box, wide-eyed. "I told Taylor to throw that box in the Dumpster where you wouldn't see it." An awkward pause followed. "I can say in all honesty that I did not buy those, Winnie. And I would also like to add that Sandie's cookies-and-cream cupcake isn't half as good as yours. I think she puts shortening in her frosting."

"Ugh." Winnie tossed the box in the trash. "Not that it really matters, but if you're ever in the mood for cupcakes, just ask."

"I will." Robin's eyes sparkled. "Since you brought it up, how about some more of those snickerdoodles?"

"This isn't my cookie day." Winnie went back to work, and Robin bolted out of the room.

Under her breath, Winnie continued to mutter something about cupcakes. Tess, looking more awake after her first cup of coffee, picked up the folder and got LuAnn's and Janice's attention. "Remember a couple of days ago when I told you all I was trying to remember something about Prudence's diary?" She opened the folder and took out her copy of the journal. "Well, I finally found it. Took me a couple of hours of searching, but I found the entry." She paused dramatically, and Janice did her best not to grab the journal from her. She'd learned you had to let Tess be Tess.

Tess set the diary down on the desk in front of her. "From the minute those messages started appearing in the bread, I had this weird, nagging feeling that I'd heard a similar story once before."

"Really?" Janice asked.

"It's in the diary," Tess explained. "Something eerily familiar." She flipped the pages, then stood and handed the diary to Janice. "Go ahead and read the entry from August 4, 1860, and see what you think."

"Okay." Janice began to read aloud from the section Tess indicated.

I turned to discover an unfamiliar man in my kitchen. He was injured, his fine clothes covered in mud and blood. Why was he lurking in the corner of my kitchen? When I asked him who he was, he stumbled and fell at my feet. I helped him to a chair and asked him once again who he was. The words he spoke bound me to him, as surely as if he'd come from heaven itself.

Janice looked up, impatient. "I don't see anything about bread in this."

Tess paced the room. "Keep reading."

Janice looked ahead to the next entry.

William left this morning on his mission. What he carries is well hidden. Anyone who stops him with sinister intentions would never guess that a loaf of bread could carry such a treasure. My prayers surely follow him to Pittsburgh and all the way back to Lexington. I also pray for the young love that unites North and South. Surely God's love calls people together, unites our differences, and joins our hearts.

"Now I've heard everything." LuAnn plopped down into the empty chair across from the desk.

"Could it be a coincidence?" Winnie asked. "Or do you think the person who planted the notes in my bread knew about all of this?"

"They had to," Tess said. "And they're capitalizing on the story."

Janice agreed. "It's got to be more than a coincidence. How many stories have you heard about something hidden in loaves of bread?"

"This would be it for me," LuAnn said.

"Me too," Tess said. "Maybe this is all some sort of weird prank."

LuAnn rubbed her forehead. "I have no idea. Unless it's a psychological trick someone is playing on us."

"And I guess we also shouldn't be surprised if Hank Clive goes to the historical society for some reason—maybe research on the inn—and finds the connection. Heaven only knows what sort of article he'll write once he knows about that." Tess groaned. "That's all we need."

Janice had been only half-listening to her friends' conversation. Something was trying to make a connection in her brain... "Hey!" she said. "Remember when we were checking on Reena's background and read about her great-great-grandmother, Birdie...oh, what was her last name?"

"Atkinson," supplied Tess.

"Yes, Atkinson." Janice waved her hand impatiently. "Anyway, wasn't she from Pittsburgh? And wasn't the man she wanted to marry from Lexington? Is that what Prudence meant by 'young love'? Could that be Birdie and the first man she was engaged to?"

"But the treasure couldn't be a note, could it?" Tess asked. "How would a note be a treasure?"

Winnie's eyes were ping-ponging between the three of them as they spoke, confusion written all over her face. "What are you all going on about?"

The phone rang, and Tess answered it. After a couple of minutes' chatter with whoever was on the other end of the line, she put her hand over the speaker and looked at Winnie. "His ears must have been burning. How would you feel about another visit from Hank Clive?"

"After what he wrote about us last time?" Winnie looked more than a little irritated. "I should think not."

"He says he's working on a new piece about the upcoming state competition, and you'll just be one of many people he's covering."

"Why won't he just leave me alone?" Winnie wailed.

"Because you're famous, that's why." LuAnn patted her on the arm. "And I think it might be interesting to know if he says anything about reading Prudence's diary."

Winnie turned to face Tess. "Tell him it's okay, but I can only give him fifteen minutes. And this time he has to say only nice things about me. Er, us."

Tess nodded, then went back to talking with Hank. She ended the call a couple of minutes later and turned to face Winnie. "Sorry about that. Hank Clive is a hard man to say no to."

Winnie waved her hand. "I'll tell him I'm too busy to talk long. That's the truth. Besides, I think we've already established he's a nosy-poke, and he has no discretion when it comes to sharing what he thinks he knows."

"I think he just wants to know which recipes you settled on for the state competition."

Winnie looked mortified by this idea. "No way! I've already told the food and travel reporter that I'm not sharing any of that information. Not until after the fact, anyway."

Tess quirked a brow. "But you have decided?"

"I have. And I'm keeping that decision to myself."

"Good for you."

Winnie grabbed an orange scone from the baking tray and put it on a small plate. "When he gets here, I'll distract him with this. Then tell him to go away."

"He'll assume you're making this for the competition."

"Let him think what he wants. You can even hint at a few of the ingredients, if you want. But I don't want to waste any time talking to someone who might take my words and use them against me in another article. Besides, I've got work to do. I've got to start thinking about Thursday's exhibit at the museum, and then I need to write down my plan of action for Saturday. It's less than a week away, Janice. I can hardly believe it."

"You've got this, Winnie." Janice offered a thumbs-up and then went to await his arrival.

A short while later, Hank arrived. He brushed through the door, a man on a mission. Janice led him into the café and gestured for him to sit at a nearby table.

"Good to see you again, Hank. I'll be right back with Winnie."

He nodded and walked over to the coffeepot.

Winnie was reluctant to leave her tasks in the kitchen, but Tess and LuAnn offered to take over. She followed Janice to the café and sat down across from Hank, placing the plate with the orange scone in front of him.

"Well, this is a nice surprise," he said. "Thanks."

"You're welcome." Winnie leaned back in the chair and gave him a dubious look. "How can I help you?"

"I have a few questions. Darla said she called you and asked about printing one of your recipes for her food and travel column."

"I told her, and I'll tell you, my recipes are secret. If things go well at the competition I'll share one, but only one."

"I see." He glanced down at the orange scone. "Is this some sort of cryptic clue?"

Winnie shrugged. "I'll leave that up to you to decide. Orange is one of my favorites. But I don't share my recipes, sorry."

"Our readers will be very disappointed."

Janice decided to interject her thoughts. "Just hang on until Winnie wins the finals in Columbus."

He glanced Janice's way. "You sound pretty sure of yourself. And her. Really think she's got the goods?"

"Mm-hmm."

He took a bite of the scone, and a delirious look came over his face. "Oh, wow. This is spectacular."

Thank goodness, the scone seemed to distract him. He kept right on eating, eyes focused on his plate. When he finished, he leaned back in his chair and reached for his napkin.

He wiped his lips and then took a swig of coffee. "Well, that hit the spot. I didn't even know I wanted or needed a scone today. Mighty good, Winnie."

"Thank you." Winnie leaned forward in her chair. "Now, how can I help you?"

"Where's Georgia this morning?"

"Georgia?" Janice and Winnie spoke in unison.

"Why?" Janice asked.

"Just curious." He took another sip of coffee. "I had a long talk with Sandie Ballard over at the Better Batter. She told me all about how she offered Georgia a job."

Chapter Eighteen

"She…what?" Janice plopped down in the chair beside Winnie and stared at Hank. "Are you sure?"

"I'm just telling you what she said. I guess she and Georgia have gotten close. I can see why. They're both young, both interested in the same things." He shrugged. "Both going places."

Winnie still looked shocked. "Georgia hasn't said a word about any of this."

"No, I suppose she hasn't." He ran his fingertip across the plate then stuck it in his mouth. "Good to the last bite."

"Well, I'll tell Georgia that you were looking for her."

He shrugged. "Hey, off the subject, but I was contacted by someone else who found a note in a loaf of your bread, Winnie."

"What? Are you sure?" Winnie's brow wrinkled.

"Was it the owner of the Sassy Seamstress, by any chance?" Janice asked.

"No." Hank's eyes widened, and he reached into his pocket for his notepad and a pencil. "She got one too?"

Well, great.

"Just wondering." Janice unfolded the napkin in front of her and refolded it. "No one else has reported in, that I know of."

"Yes, and if you think for one minute that I'm somehow to blame for all of that, think again," Winnie said. "I'm rarely in that kitchen alone these days. Not that I would ever do anything to hurt the reputation of these ladies or this inn. Those notes are a thing of the past."

"Oh, really? Take a look at this, then. See for yourself." He reached into his pocket and came out with his wallet, which he opened. He pulled out a pink laminated slip of paper.

Janice leaned down to read the words typed on the slip. *Great harm will come to you if you stay at Wayfarers Inn.*

This stopped Janice in her tracks. "Whoa. You're saying you know the person who received this note?"

"Sure do. Can't divulge the name, though."

Janice's frustrations grew as she observed the smirk on Hank's face. "The police will need to know the name of the person. Have you called Officer Randy Lewis at Marietta PD?"

"Sorry, but I won't reveal my sources."

"Even to the police?"

"Even to the police."

Janice released a slow breath and tried to overcome the feelings of anger that threatened to rise to the surface.

"I know who got what," Winnie said. "It's all easy enough to figure out."

"Yes," Janice concurred. "A few of the original recipients have already come to us personally, and we've made good on our offer." She didn't tell him that most turned her down and also canceled their reservations. Janice tried to look confident as she added, "We'll go through the list of who's left and make sure everyone's covered." She stared at Hank. "And for the record, I don't see why you won't just tell us who gave you that note. We're all on the same team here."

"Are we?" Hank took a final swig of his coffee, pushed the chair back, and reached for his wallet. "What do I owe you for the scone?"

"This one's on the house," Janice said.

"You sure?" He looked perplexed by her generosity.

"Yep." Winnie turned and walked back toward the kitchen, muttering under her breath.

"Well, then." He gave Janice a curt nod, then turned and left.

"Not even a thank-you." Janice sighed. "For a scone that good, you'd think he would at least say thanks."

Janice did her best to act normal as Reena entered the room. This morning's ensemble was a bright orange number with vibrant flowers. Even the shoes were orange. Tess and LuAnn would love this.

Robin entered the café behind her, broom in hand.

"I'm not one to gossip, but that fella gives me a bad feeling." Reena gestured in the direction Hank had gone.

"Me too," Robin said. "From the first time I met him something struck me as odd. But that's just me, mind you. I get weird vibes around people sometimes." She propped the broom up next to the wall. "I know we're supposed to be gracious to everyone, but every time he comes around I just feel like swatting him with a flyswatter. What sort of person looks to profit off of someone else's misfortune?" Before Janice could respond, Robin added, "A low-down, no good person, that's who."

"We don't really know that he's lowdown," Janice countered. "He's just out for a story."

"Or making up a story."

"And another thing," Reena interjected. "Why doesn't he shave? He always looks unkempt, like he hasn't seen a razor in days."

"I don't know." Janice pushed the chairs back in around the table and then grabbed the dirty plate. "A lot of guys are going around like that these days—scraggly looking. I'm not a fan, but who am I to judge such things? I'm a little stymied about why he shaves his head but not his face. If you've got time for one, I'd think you'd have time for the other."

"That's a question that I simply cannot answer." Robin started sweeping under the table. "You would have to ask the man himself."

"Never in a million years." Janice laughed. "I guess I'll just go on speculating."

Reena shuffled across the room and took a spot at an empty table. Janice filled a mug with coffee and set it in front of her.

Robin continued to sweep. "Well, since we're assessing his looks, I'm guessing he's single."

"And you're basing that on...what?" Janice asked.

Robin's nose wrinkled. "He's pencil-thin. I've had skinless chicken with more fat on it than that. If he had a wife, he'd be plumper."

Janice decided it was time to head back into the kitchen to help Winnie. She found Tess seated at the table, updating the lunch menu. Tess glanced her way as Janice entered the room.

"So, Winnie brought me up to date on Hank." She posed the words more as a question than a statement.

"Yes." Janice nodded. "He didn't mention anything about Prudence or her journal, or even going to the historical society, for that matter. I managed to get rid of him in short order, but he was definitely in the café with a cup of coffee and an orange scone."

"Or was he in the drawing room with a candlestick?" Winnie asked. "I can't remember."

"Point is, he showed up looking for another story," Janice said. "I still don't trust the guy. And I'm not the only one who finds him suspect. Reena and Robin are leery of him too."

"Me too." Winnie turned away from her work to give her a solid nod. "There's something about the guy that sets the hairs on my arms to standing up. I can't pinpoint it, but he's different."

"I wonder why they have him covering local stories like the baking competition," Tess said. "I would think they'd put him on national news or something like that."

Janice nodded. "There's something to be said for getting bad vibes from a person."

"Bad vibes do not a suspect make." Tess rose from her spot at the table. "The guy's a little intrusive, but I don't see any other reason to be suspicious of him."

Janice continued to wipe down the sticky work surfaces in the kitchen but found herself distracted. She couldn't stop thinking about Hank Clive and how he kept turning up, looking for a story. The man had impeccable timing.

Or would that be suspicious timing?

The more she thought about it, the more she wondered. Had he come to Wayfarers Inn to get a story—or to chronicle one he had instigated?

Before she could give the matter further thought, Georgia entered the kitchen from the mudroom.

"Good morning, sleepyhead," Winnie said with a smile. "Glad you could join us."

"I'm so grateful for the extra sleep." Georgia set her purse down on a chair and faced the ladies. "But it looks like I arrived just in time for some excitement."

"Excitement?" Tess asked.

"Oh, you mean Hank Clive showing up to ask more questions?" Janice added.

Creases formed between Georgia's brows. "Are you saying he's already been in here?"

"Yes," Janice and Winnie said in unison.

"Weird. He was hanging around out back when I got here."

"But Hank left several minutes ago," Winnie said.

"I saw it with my own eyes," Janice added.

"Then something must've made him turn around, because I promise you, the guy was standing by the back door, scribbling something in that notebook of his." She turned toward the door. "Let me go check and see if he's still here."

She returned a moment later. "Nope, he's gone. I looked both ways but didn't see him."

A little shiver ran down Janice's spine. Regardless of his motives, Hank Clive had no business hanging around the back of the inn. He was definitely up to something.

CHAPTER NINETEEN

On Tuesday afternoon, Winnie barely came out of the kitchen. She worked long and hard, preparing for Thursday's exhibit. Janice was worried about her—as she had been for many days now—but couldn't seem to stop the woman from pouring herself into her work. She seemed a bit grumpy, which threw the whole inn into a state of irritability.

Janice encountered the sourest attitude in Robin, who fussed and fumed as she changed sheets on the bed in Apples and Cinnamon.

Janice stuck her head in the door and watched for a moment before asking, "We aren't overworking you, are we, Robin? I counted, and we only have five rooms in use this weekend. Is everything okay?"

Robin yanked the fitted sheet off the bed and groaned. Loudly. "I love working at the inn, Janice. You know that. But things are so much easier when everyone is in a good mood."

"Referring to Winnie?"

"Yes. It's hardly fair that the rest of us have to suffer because Winnie's in a grumpy mood."

"I'm sorry, Robin."

She shrugged, then pulled a pillowcase off a pillow. "I'll be glad when the finals are behind us. Everyone's in an uproar over a dumb contest."

"I'd hardly call it dumb."

"Well, you know what I mean." She tossed the pillowcase into the pile of linens on the floor. "Nothing is the same right now. And you see what it's done to our guests, right? Folks are running away from Wayfarers like we're some sort of haunted house. A lady at the supermarket told me that she got a really nasty note in her loaf of bread. When I asked her what it said, she told me she couldn't say in front of the children, for fear of scaring them."

"Oh dear."

"Right?" Robin sat on the edge of the bed. "It's just sad. People all over town are twisted up over this message in a bottle story." She sighed and reached for the other pillow. "I mean, messages in bread. Same idea, though, I guess."

"Yes, only we had nothing to do with those messages. You do believe that, don't you, Robin?"

"Of course I do." She paused and wrinkled her nose. "At least I don't think any of you had anything to do with it. But I can't rule out *everyone* in the inn."

"Who do you suspect?"

"I'm just saying, that Georgia-chick has been acting weird." Robin lowered her voice. "She slips in and out, and she certainly had access to the kitchen on the day the bread was baked. I never really trusted her from the beginning."

"Why is that?"

"She's a...what's the word?" Robin paused and appeared to be thinking. "An interloper."

"Interloper?"

"Yeah, that's the word folks use whenever someone over-stays their welcome. Georgia shows up from out of nowhere and wants to be adopted into the family? Who does that? I mean, I did that. But still!"

"I see." Was that a note of jealousy in Robin's voice, per-haps? Did she really mistrust Georgia, or was she simply jeal-ous of the amount of attention the young woman received from everyone else at the inn?

Janice headed downstairs. Reena was sitting in the café—and she seemed to be in a pretty cranky mood as well. Hopefully that had nothing to do with Winnie. Janice refilled Reena's coffee and offered her a crossword puzzle to work.

Janice was headed to the lobby when she was greeted by Kip and the little stray pup, who wore a proper collar and leash. "We're back!"

Georgia entered the café with a tray of cookies in hand. She took one look at Kip and smiled. "Oh, hello. Did you bring this little fellow to see me?"

Kip nodded. "Yes, I wanted to show you how far he's come." Kip told the dog to sit, and the pup followed the command right away. Kip beamed. "I've been working with him. He's a smart little guy. He's already conquered sit and stay."

"Smart and cute," Janice said. "I'm afraid we still can't take him though," she added sorrowfully.

The smile on his face faded. "Oh, I know. Hope you don't think I meant it that way. I just stopped by to tell you that I took him to the vet. He's had his first round of shots, and they scanned him for a microchip. He doesn't have one."

Reena called from her table. "Is that little monster back? I thought you got rid of him. And what's he doing in the café?"

"He's not staying," Kip explained. "I just came by to give you guys a heads-up. The vet confirmed he's a chiweenie. That's half Chihuahua and half wiener dog."

"Both breeds notoriously yappy." Reena rolled her eyes. "But then again, what do I know? I've never been one for dogs, that's for sure." She adjusted her position in her chair and continued to work on her crossword puzzle.

Kip turned his attention to Georgia and Janice. "Actually, the vet said that Dobbins here will end up being the perfect lapdog. Just the right size and completely dedicated to his owner."

"Wait, 'Dobbins'?" Janice shook her head. "Who's Dobbins?"

"Oh, sorry." Kip laughed. "Figured he needed to be named after another one of Twain's characters to fit in around here."

"The right owner will come along soon." Janice leaned down to scratch the little pooch behind the ears. "He might be active, but he's a cutie. Hopefully it won't take you long to find the right person to adopt him."

"Right. I'd keep him myself if my schedule wasn't so crazy." Kip shrugged. "For now, I'm just happy to foster him and give him some training during my off hours." Kip turned his attention to Georgia. "Actually, I also came by to bring you something. Remember that book we were talking about the other day?"

Georgia nodded, and her eyes sparkled. "Sure do. *Heaven's Prize.*"

"I stumbled across a copy at the half-price bookstore, so I picked it up. Thought you might like it."

"Really?" She clasped her hands together. "I've been dying to read it."

"I know."

"What is *Heaven's Prize*?" Janice asked. "Never heard of it."

"It's a novel that's on the *New York Times* Best Sellers list," Georgia explained. "I was telling Kip how much I adore Madeline O'Shea, the author, and he picked up a copy of the book for me. I'm super grateful." She smiled warmly at Kip, then knelt down on the floor in front of the pup, who got so excited that he left a tiny puddle on the entryway floor.

"I'll clean up the mess," Georgia offered, and went in search of the mop.

"And I'll take him outside." Kip patted the little pup on the head. "But first, let me get that book. I left it in the car."

He passed the leash off to Janice. She scratched the little dog behind the ears again as Georgia arrived with the mop to clean up the piddle spot. Just as Georgia finished, a delivery woman entered the lobby with a package. She came into the café and spotted Dobbins, who greeted her with tail wagging.

"I just love chiweenies!" the woman exclaimed. "I had one as a girl."

"Oh?" Janice held tight to the leash.

"Yes, my aunt used to breed them. They're such sweet little things, but so active. And skittish too. But they make great family pets."

Janice did her best to hold on to the pup, but after a while she got tired of the tugging and let him go to the delivery woman. Hopefully the little imp would behave himself as he sat at her feet.

A couple of minutes later, a loud crash sounded from behind them. Janice looked down at the spot where a puppy used to be and whipped around.

A chaotic sight met her. A broken plate lay on the floor next to Reena's table. Dobbins sat on her lap, licking her cheek.

"Oh no!" Janice rushed her way. "What in the world?"

Reena shook her head and pointed at the dog. "This horrible little beast attacked me!"

"I'm sure he didn't mean to attack you, Reena," Georgia said as she scooped the pup into her arms. "Maybe he just finds you irresistible."

"Right. Maybe he just wanted to sit in your lap," Janice suggested.

"I was half-asleep, wondering if anyone was ever going to notice me sitting here eating a cookie and working this ridiculous crossword puzzle, when all of a sudden . . . *bam!* Something landed on me and knocked the breath out of me. Next thing you know, I was being kissed."

Janice suppressed a sigh and turned her attention to Georgia. "Georgia, could you take care of the dog, please? And whatever happened to Kip? I thought he was taking the pup with him."

"He is," Georgia explained. "He just ran out to the car to get that book for me. Sorry, Janice."

"It's not your fault." Janice reached over to pet the hyper little pup. "This little fella is really sweet."

"Sweet, my eye. He's a menace." Reena settled back into her chair. She pointed to the table. "First he jumped into my lap, then he ate my snickerdoodles."

"Oh no!" Georgia squealed. "Dogs can't have cinnamon!"

Reena shook her finger in Georgia's direction. "Forget the cinnamon, that mongrel ate my sweet treat. I brought those down from my room, just in case Winnie didn't have time to bake today."

"I'm so sorry, Miss Reena," Georgia said. "And I'm also sorry about the mess he made. I'll clean it up."

Reena brushed her hands against her slacks and used her napkin to wipe down the table. "I'll move to another table. Doesn't look like we've got any other guests coming, anyway." Her gaze traveled from one end of the empty café to the other. "And I suppose I'll just start over with a new treat. What else does Winnie have in that kitchen of hers?"

"I'll look, Reena. Please don't worry. I'll find something for you to nibble on." Janice sighed and walked into the kitchen.

"Everything okay out there?" Winnie asked from her spot in front of Big Red. She looked up from the pot of stew she had been stirring.

"No. The dog ate Reena's snickerdoodle."

"Huck?" LuAnn and Winnie asked in unison.

"Definitely not. It was that little Chihuahua-wiener-thing that showed up last week. Kip brought him by for a visit and passed him off to me. I fell down on the job. Next thing you know, he jumped up on Reena's lap, knocked her plate to the floor, and ate her cookies. Then he licked her right on the face."

"Hey, that dog knows a good cookie when he sees one." LuAnn chuckled. "But I'm guessing the ornery Reena wasn't as sweet."

"Right. Point is, Reena wants a redo on dessert. So, what else do we have?"

"I've got a lemon-berry pie cooling on the counter over there." Winnie pointed. "That will have to do. I don't have time for anything else."

"Well, since it's just Reena, I think we're safe."

"Are we ever really safe with Reena Newberry?" LuAnn quirked a brow.

Janice couldn't help but laugh. She reached for a knife to slice the pie, but a noise on the far side of the room interrupted her thoughts.

"Whew!" Georgia said from the doorway. "I'm so relieved. Turns out cinnamon isn't a problem for dogs. It's nutmeg." She gave Winnie a warning look. "You didn't put nutmeg in those cookies, did you, Winnie? I can't remember."

"In a snickerdoodle? Of course not. But even if I had, I wouldn't be responsible for that dog's health and well-being.

I didn't tell the little monster to eat Reena Newberry's lunch."

"He didn't eat her lunch, just her dessert," Georgia said, "but I still haven't figured out what to give Reena as a replacement. Anyone have any ideas?"

"I'm slicing this lemon-berry pie for her," Janice explained. "Give me a minute, and I'll take it out to her. But I want to let it cool a bit first."

"She's pretty impatient." Georgia glanced Winnie's way. "Do you have some other sort of cookie, maybe?"

"Nope. I do have some chocolate cupcakes in the cupboard. I happen to know she loves chocolate."

"Perfect. That should hit the spot."

"Georgia, you just make sure that dog isn't anywhere nearby or—" Janice turned to discover Georgia had left the room. "What in the world? Wasn't she just here?"

"That girl has all of a sudden started disappearing on me." Winnie groaned and tended to the vegetables in the oven.

"Seriously? She's falling down on the job?"

"Not sure I'd put it that way, but she disappeared on me this morning for a little while. It was so odd. She was right there working with me one minute, and gone the next."

"Bathroom break?" Janice tried.

Winnie shrugged. "If so, she's suffering some sort of ailment. She was gone a good half hour. Then when she turned back up again she got right back to work, as if nothing had happened."

"Maybe she got a call from her dad," Janice suggested. "I know when he called the other day he said that her younger siblings are really missing her. They probably wanted to chat."

"Yes, but when she knows I'm so busy? Her timing is definitely off. Not very considerate to keep taking off."

"That is a little strange." Janice paused to think about it. "Do you think I should talk to her?"

"No." Winnie shook her head. "I'll have a little chat with her later."

Georgia entered the room looking a bit perplexed. "Sorry, didn't mean to eavesdrop, but I heard my name. Did I do something wrong?" She reached for an apple, brushed it against the edge of her T-shirt, and took a bite.

"No, nothing wrong," Winnie said, then pointed at the mound of pie crust dough. "I was hoping you could roll that out for me so we can get these coconut cream pies going."

"You want me to roll out your pie crust? Are you serious?" Georgia's bright blue eyes widened in obvious surprise. "Are you sure?"

"Of course. It's about time you learned to do that. But wash those hands of yours. I know you've been petting that dog."

"Kip just left with Dobbins. He's such a sweetheart."

Janice looked at Georgia and wondered if the bubbly young woman was talking about the dog... or the boy.

CHAPTER TWENTY

August 5, 1860

William was astride his horse the next morning just as he'd said, at first light. The bread, with the ring inside, was wrapped and stowed safely in his saddlebag. Prudence had checked his wounds and warned him to keep the bandages clean and dry.

She looked up at him as he gathered his reins. "Don't forget, William, thee is welcome to rest here on thy way back home. We would be glad to see thee again."

"That is very kind of thee, Prudence," said William. "It is not likely that I shall ever forget how thee and Jason were the answer to my prayers." He held out his hand, and she shook it. "The Lord has truly gifted thee with abundant intelligence."

Jason laughed. "William," he said, "I am a very blessed man. Not only is my wife intelligent and resourceful, she is, as thee knows, kind and generous." He took his turn shaking William's hand. "She is also a godly woman. I can promise thee that thy name will be in her prayers long after thee reaches Pittsburgh and returns to thy home in Lexington."

"I believe thee," William said fervently. "I will try to get word to thee of my success." He wheeled his horse around. "In the meantime, be assured of my prayers also for both of thee."

In just a few moments all that was left of William's visit was a cloud of dust above the road. "Go with God," Prudence whispered.

CHAPTER TWENTY-ONE

On Thursday morning, the Inn Crowd left Reena in Robin's care and headed out to the historical society to cheer Winnie on. Brad met them at the front door, all smiles.

"Ready to roll, Winnie?" he asked.

She offered a terrified nod.

He opened the door and ushered them inside. Well, most of them. Winnie seemed to be frozen in place. Janice could tell she was nervous about going inside. She didn't blame her.

"You okay?" Brad asked after a moment.

"I'm nervous folks will still be talking about those notes they found in the bread," Winnie said. "Can't believe I'm stopping everything to do this, and so close to the competition too."

"It's going to be fun." Janice patted her on the arm.

LuAnn wrapped her arms around Winnie in a tender hug. "We're so proud of you, Winnie. You're really the best. That's why they've asked for you. Now come on in." She took Winnie by the hand, and she stepped through the door.

Once inside, tears sprang to Winnie's eyes. "I'm not, though. Don't you see? I'm not the best, and I'm tired of feeling like I have to prove that I am. I just want to go back to being plain old Winnie, who cooks for Wayfarers Inn."

"You've never been plain old Winnie to any of us," Brad said.

"Yes, that's right," Janice agreed. "And soon things really will slow down. This will all be a distant memory."

"Just get this behind you, Winnie," Brad said. "Then you can focus on getting past the competition so your life can go back to normal."

Winnie responded with a concerned frown.

They were met inside by Emma Carpenter, a friend they had once fondly referred to as Polka-Dot. The young woman was bubbling with excitement.

"I can't believe the exhibit is today." She gave Winnie a big hug. "Everyone is so excited, Winnie. I told Margaret that I would volunteer today, just so I could see you in action. It's going to be great." She continued to bubble over as she walked the ladies into the event.

When they reached the exhibit, Winnie's frown flipped upside down right away. "Will you look at that?" She pointed to an 1850s farm kitchen cookstove, then to the next stove and the next. The area also featured all sorts of pots and pans from that era, as well as plates and coffee mugs.

Janice could hardly believe the amazing display items Margaret had come up with, particularly the main stove. What a beauty. And so practical too. With one device, a pioneer wife could bake, cook beans, and roast a chicken, all while keeping her house warm. Fascinating. It felt as if they had all stepped back in time. She could almost picture what it must have been like back in Prudence's day. If only these ovens could talk! What amazing stories they would tell.

As they walked through the exhibit, Janice caught a glimpse of Hank Clive talking to Margaret. He had that same gray notepad open and appeared to be taking notes. Ugh. Hopefully he would report on this event without any sort of slant.

"Of course, *he* would be here," Tess said. "I can only imagine the story he's jotting down right now. Something negative about Winnie or the inn, no doubt."

"Maybe he's just here to cover the exhibit," LuAnn said.

"Or maybe he has a little crush on Sandie Ballard," Tess suggested. "Has anyone thought of that? Maybe he's keen on painting Winnie in a bad light to make Sandie look better. Maybe he thinks he can win her if he takes down her opponent."

"Well, Sandie's not Winnie's opponent today," Janice reminded them. "They're working together, remember?"

"I think it'll be good for the people of Marietta to see them as a team," Tess said.

Janice agreed but still had some lingering doubts about Sandie.

"I'll go over and have a chat with Hank," Brad said. "That's one of the reasons I came today, to be honest, to keep an eye on him. That last article of his sent my radar up."

"Good, Brad." Winnie patted him on the hand. "Please go over there and tell him I said to behave."

A smile tugged at the edges of Brad's lips. "Yes, ma'am. I'm on it." He took off through the crowd and disappeared from view.

Margaret appeared and gave Winnie some last-minute instructions, then led her up to the wood cookstove and explained how to use it. Winnie unloaded her supplies, double-checked her bread dough to make sure it was still in good shape, and set up her work space.

A few minutes before the event was set to begin, Sandie Ballard arrived. She clasped her hands together and exclaimed, "Oh, my goodness! Winnie Washington! I'm so excited to work with you." She bounded into the exhibit area and gave Winnie a huge hug. "I haven't seen you since the competition and haven't had a chance to tell you how proud I am of you."

"You...you are?" Winnie did not look convinced.

"Of course. Girl, I have a lot to learn from you. That's why I'm so excited about today's event."

"Really?" Winnie still had a dubious look on her face.

"Yes, I am." Sandie gushed over Winnie for a few more minutes, then set up her workstation with baking pans, bread dough, and other items of interest.

Once the two women were ready to go, Janice looked around for Georgia. She must have taken off through the crowd. Odd.

In that moment, Janice remembered what Hank had told her just the other day, that Sandie had offered Georgia a job. Was Georgia hiding out, hoping Winnie wouldn't discover her secret?

Janice craned her neck to have a better look around the room. Hopefully Georgia would return before the baking began. She needed to offer Winnie her moral support, if nothing else.

"Who are you looking for, Janice?" Tess asked.

"Georgia."

LuAnn looked to the right and then the left. "Did she really just disappear on us again?"

Janice nodded.

"Something about that girl is starting to trouble me," LuAnn said.

"Maybe we should be even more troubled than we already are." Janice told her friends what Hank had shared with her about Sandie offering Georgia a job.

Tess looked flabbergasted by this news. "Do you think that's really true?"

Janice shrugged. "I have no reason to doubt him." She shifted her gaze to the exhibit. "On the other hand, Sandie seems to be really nice. Today, anyway. So the whole thing has me confused."

Tess leaned over and stage-whispered, "I haven't come out and asked this question, but do you think there's any chance whatsoever that Georgia is the one who put the notes in the bread?"

"She's given me cause for concern," Janice said. "But the more I get to know her, the more I think she's the real deal. Of course, there are some unanswered questions in my mind about her chat with Sandie."

"Right." Tess shrugged. "I don't know. I guess that's the point. We don't really know her very well, do we? I just know that she's Georgia from Akron, and she seems to like to bake. Maybe she's really someone else altogether. I mean, remember how it was with Kylie? We didn't suspect her either, but she ended up being out to get LuAnn. Maybe the same thing is true here. Maybe Georgia was sent to spy on the inn or to bring us down."

LuAnn shook her head. "You sound like a conspiracy theorist, Tess. Georgia's great. I've really gotten to know her. She adores Winnie, so I can't imagine she would do anything to hurt her."

"Right. But what if all of that is a ruse of some sort? What if we were set up?"

"I think she really is who she says she is. And I'm not surprised that Sandie would offer her a job. We're not paying her for the work she's doing at the inn, so why would it be traitorous for her to think about taking a paying job? Maybe she's thinking of getting some practical experience before she returns to school. Anyway, I think she's completely enamored with cooking and with Winnie."

"Speaking of Winnie..." Janice pointed to the stage. "Looks like Margaret is introducing her."

Sure enough, Margaret took a microphone in hand and introduced Winnie as Marietta's own Rising Star. When Winnie stepped forward to take the mic, a rousing, "Go, Winnie!" rang out from the back of the room. Sounded like Kip's voice.

Janice turned and noticed that Georgia was standing next to him. The young woman hollered, "Winnie for the win!" and then whistled—one of those shrill fingers-in-the-mouth whistles.

Winnie offered a nervous wave to her fans and began her speech. "I want to start by thanking the fine people of Marietta for supporting me. We've had our ups and downs over the past couple of weeks, but I just keep doing my best to take things one day at a time. I'll be competing in Columbus, day after tomorrow, and I'd like to ask you all to pray for me, if you will—not that I would win, but that I will do my very best. That's all I can ask, after all."

"You are the best!" Kip called out.

Janice couldn't help but notice Sandie Ballard's face contort. This must be hard, to hear so much praise for her opponent.

On the other hand, Sandie didn't seem to be in competition mode today. When Winnie finished her speech, Sandie gave a rousing cheer and then welcomed the crowd to watch them work together. Winnie fired up the woodstove and then they got busy shaping their dough and putting it into pans.

The crowd continued to watch as the two bakers put their pans into the oven. While the bread baked, Winnie gave some tips on troubleshooting common bread-making problems. She was right in the middle of discussing varieties of yeast when a plume of smoke and flames shot out of the stove. Sandie screamed, and Winnie grabbed her by the shoulders and pulled her off the stage.

Shrill chirping filled the room as the smoke detectors went off, and people began to rush toward the door. Janice watched, pressed in by the crowd, as Margaret raced toward the ovens, fire extinguisher in hand. Seconds later, the flames were squelched. Smoke continued to fill the room, making it difficult to breathe.

Janice made her way through the crowd to where Winnie stood, mouth agape, tears in her eyes.

"I don't know what happened." Her voice was trembling, and her hands were shaking.

"It's not your fault, Winnie." Margaret continued to spray the stove with the extinguisher. "You didn't do anything wrong. You followed my instructions to a T. I don't understand how that could have happened. I had Justin from the fire department come and check the stoves out."

Janice agreed—it wasn't Winnie's fault. The age of the stove had likely caused this incident. But as she watched Sandie stand frozen in place, as she took in Hank Clive's frantic note-taking, she had to wonder if, perhaps, someone had sabotaged that oven.

A couple of minutes later most of the audience had left the building. Besides their group, only Hank remained, still scribbling notes and taking photos with his camera. If he'd come looking for a story, he certainly had one now.

Kip and Georgia joined them in the exhibit area. The concern in Georgia's eyes was undeniable. She ran toward Winnie and engulfed her in a hug.

"Are you okay, Winnie?"

"I—I think so." But she sure didn't look okay.

Georgia turned her attention to Sandie, who'd bolted from the building like a rabbit shooting down its hole. But why? Janice would have to ask Georgia about that later. For now, they needed to tend to Winnie.

Janice put her arm around Winnie and led her to a nearby stool. "Here, Winnie, sit down." She kept her arm around Winnie's shoulders. "Can I get you anything? A drink maybe?"

Winnie shook her head. "No, please don't. There's been enough excitement as it is. The last thing I need is that reporter over there seeing me get fussed over. I'll never live that down."

"Did anyone see what happened to Sandie?" Margaret looked around as the smoke cleared. "I think she disappeared on us. I just need to make sure she's okay. She was standing awfully close to those flames. That was quick thinking on your part, Winnie, to get her out of there."

"She left when she saw me," Georgia said.

"Why would she do that?" This question came from LuAnn.

"Yes, why would she do that?" Janice echoed.

Georgia released a sigh. "I guess it's time I shared something with you all." She looked at Winnie. "I didn't want to tell you, but Sandie offered me a job a while back."

"Well, isn't that something?" Winnie said.

"I know. I couldn't believe it either. I told her right away that I was going back to school so it was out of the question. She was very kind about it, but said if I ever changed my mind…"

"Which you won't do, I hope." Winnie frowned. "School is very important."

"Right. I have no intention of quitting school. She asked if I wanted to work for her the rest of the month, but I said no. I told her the whole reason I came here was to learn from you."

"Well, we appreciate you telling us this, Georgia," Tess said. "Better to have things out in the open, I always say."

"Right. I thought it would be best to let you know." Georgia paused. "I love you, Winnie. You know that, right?"

Winnie's eyes immediately brimmed with tears. "Love you too, girlie. And just for the record, I wouldn't blame you if you wanted to work for Sandie the last couple of weeks you're here. From everything I've heard, she's got a really sweet bakery, probably right up your alley."

"Why would I ever need to do that?" Georgia looked genuinely perplexed by this notion. "I've got you."

"Just out of curiosity, when did Sandie ask you this?" Janice asked.

Georgia's eyes narrowed. "I think it was the day Winnie was doing all of her bread baking. You remember—the day before the banner went up. Anyway, I saw her lurking outside the kitchen door and asked if I could help her. She told me she had been watching me assist you during the competition and could tell that I loved to bake. I guess she was trying to entice me, because she brought a bag of sweets with her when she came."

Ah, so that explained the bakery bag.

"What happened to them, Georgia?" Janice asked. "Surely you didn't eat them all."

"Of course not. In fact, I didn't even look inside the bag." She turned to Winnie and said, "I'm sorry. I should've just told you."

"This is all so strange," Winnie said. "If she left a bag of sweets, what happened to them?"

"I feel bad about it now," Georgia said, "but I tossed the whole bag in the Dumpster as soon as she left."

"So there goes my theory that she might have brought several loaves of her own bread to swap out with yours, Winnie." Janice shrugged.

"That would have been a bit of a stretch." Winnie folded her arms over her chest. "She just happened to show up when I was out of the kitchen. She just happened to know that I had baked that morning. She just happened to know how many loaves to prepare for this big swap, and she just happened to pull this over on all of us while we were all at the inn working?" Winnie shook her head. "Sorry, but that's all a little too coincidental for me. I'm not saying it's impossible; I'm just saying it's improbable."

Janice couldn't help but agree. Her earlier theory now sounded completely farfetched. "I guess my sleuthing skills are slipping."

"No, I'd say we've eliminated a suspect," Tess said. "Which means we're getting closer to knowing who really did put the notes in the bread. So don't give up now."

True. Janice paused to think through what she'd just learned. Maybe Sandie really had come by the inn that day just to try to steal Georgia away. Thank goodness, it hadn't worked. Georgia was now part of their team and appeared to be happy about it.

Out of the corner of her eye Janice caught a glimpse of Hank Clive taking another photo of the whole group of them. Lovely. No doubt they would all end up on the front page of tomorrow's *Times*. But what kind of story would he come up with this time?

CHAPTER TWENTY-TWO

A storm blew in on Friday morning. It seemed to set the mood for everyone at the inn. They had closed the café until Monday morning in preparation for the competition. Winnie was under enough stress without the added pressure of feeding guests. Janice managed to snag the morning paper before anyone else saw it. She slipped into the office for some alone time. As she had feared, this morning's edition of the *Marietta Times* featured an article about the fire at the exhibit and cast suspicion on Winnie as the culprit of a prank gone wrong. There, top and center of the front page, was a picture of Winnie, surrounded by concerned friends, looking as if she were going to faint.

The image was almost more than Janice could take. She fussed and fumed all morning, wishing she had the courage to pick up the phone and call Hank Clive to give him a piece of her mind. Oh, the things she would say! How dare he blame that fire on Winnie? How dare he publish a picture of Winnie at her lowest? And how dare he continue this barrage of insults against the inn?

By ten o'clock Janice had finally decided to visit him in person at the *Marietta Times*. No more pussyfooting around. It was time to speak the truth.

Janice invited Tess and LuAnn to go along with her. Better to present a strong front, especially when they planned to meet Hank Clive on his own turf. Georgia and Kip caught wind of their plans and asked if they could come too.

"We'll just wait in the lobby," Kip explained. "That way we'll be close by if you need us."

They arrived at the *Times* office at exactly eleven fifteen. They came with no invitation in hand. The summer rainstorm above them seemed an adequate representation of their mood as Janice pulled her car into the parking lot.

"You say he doesn't know we're coming?" LuAnn asked as she gazed at the building. "You sure that's wise?"

"I decided a surprise attack would be best. I don't want him to know until we walk into his office. That way he's not prepared with some sort of speech."

Tess reached for her umbrella and swung the back door open. "Well, here goes nothing. Let's just hope he's not out researching some big story."

It turned out, he wasn't. Hank, who seemed a bit surprised to see them, ushered the trio into his office the moment he heard they had arrived. He gestured for them to sit, but unfortunately there were only two chairs opposite his desk. Janice told her friends to take the seats. Standing would give her the courage required to accomplish the task for which she'd come.

Hank took a seat in his worn office chair, then leaned back with his hands behind his head. "To what do I owe the honor, ladies?"

Janice drew in a deep breath, ready to get this show on the road. She found herself distracted by his messy office. It was a lot to take in. The desk was a jumble of papers, stacked this way and that, all interspersed with books and brochures of local sites. A small bookshelf on the far wall held volumes of Encyclopedia Britannica that must be forty years old, if such a thing could be judged from the layers of dust covering them. Atop the desk, a vase with a withered plant begged for mercy. It was all she could do not to go in search of a watering can.

"I hope you don't mind that we dropped in like this," Janice said, after giving the room a thorough look.

"Of course not. I'm happy to have you."

She decided a little small talk was in order to break the ice. "Looks like you're a reader." Janice gestured to his desk, stacked high with history and travel books.

He sat up straight in his chair. "That would be putting it mildly."

Tess leaned forward in her chair and took one of the brochures in hand. "If you want to know anything about the area, just ask. You can only learn so much from reading. I always say if you want a story you have to go straight to the source."

"Funny, that sounds like something I'd say." He pursed his lips and appeared to be embarrassed by her offer to help. "I find the books and brochures helpful. And I've already made the rounds to several of the businesses in this area to learn what I can firsthand."

"You're settling in well, then?"

"Yes." He leaned back in his chair and put his hands behind his head once again. "But why do I get the feeling you ladies have come for more than an inquiry about my health and well-being?"

Janice offered up a silent prayer for courage and then dove in. "Hank, we've come to talk with you about these articles you've been writing about Winnie."

"What about them?" He looked genuinely confused.

"They're riddled with exaggerations and inaccuracies," Tess chimed in. "It's as if you take a strand of truth, exaggerate it, and then add your own fictional elements. It's hardly fair to her or to the inn."

"I'm not paid to promote your inn. The *Times* pays me to tell stories."

"But you're blowing these stories up and making them sensational when they're simply not." LuAnn's chair squeaked underneath her.

"Oh, but they are sensational. How often do you hear a story about someone planting secret messages in loaves of bread? This is a first for me."

Okay, then. Maybe he hadn't read Prudence's diary, after all. That notion brought Janice some degree of comfort. Or maybe he was just saying all of this to throw them off-track.

"Besides," Hank said, "I already have a title in mind for my next article. 'Wayfarers Inn's Secret Ingredient.'"

Janice clenched her fists. "That's not fair," she said vehemently.

"We're concerned that you've made a particular target out of Winnie," LuAnn said. "And the inn, for that matter. I'd say we're dealing with a case of libel here."

"Libel?" He laughed. Just as quickly, his brow knitted. "Are you serious?"

"Very." LuAnn leaned back in her chair and crossed her arms over her chest.

"Now, why would I care about your little inn?" For the first time since their arrival, Hank looked genuinely irritated.

"We're not asking you to care," Janice said. "Just to be fair. Before you write about the inn, come and stay as our guest. Wayfarers Inn has plenty of secrets to uncover, but they're not the ones you're writing about."

"Yes, I'm well aware of many of your secrets." He leaned forward and put his elbows on the desk. "I did my research about the inn, Ms. Eastman. I know that it was a stop on the Underground Railroad."

Okay, so maybe he had read Prudence's diary after all.

"I'm glad you've done your research. There have been plenty of articles in the *Times* about us already," she countered, "but if you ever want a fresh angle, just ask. We've got lots of stories, true ones. One doesn't have to search far for an angle when it comes to Wayfarers Inn."

"Especially these days." He squinted and then leaned back in his chair. "I'd say there's as much drama going on at the inn now as ever, though I understand from my research that it was always a place of interest."

"I would hardly say there's as much drama as ever. After all, history has proven that the inn was in the business of saving lives."

"A reputation you would never want to see sullied." His square jaw tensed visibly.

Okay, what was that all about? Was he just being mean, or did Hank Clive have some sort of trick up his sleeve?

"I know all about the diary and the woman who wrote it," he said. "You see, ladies, I've done my homework. I've researched it well and have drawn my own conclusions about the inn's history."

Why did he say that with a tightly knitted brow?

Janice decided a more businesslike approach was in order. Her next words came out sounding like an advertisement. "The inn has a marvelous reputation in town, and we'd like to keep it that way, which is why we've stopped by. We are hoping you'll resist any further temptation to write stories that paint the inn in a bad light."

"Oh, you are, are you?" His eyes shimmered with mischief. "I was wondering why you stopped by. Now I see."

"I'm sure you wouldn't want to have your reputation tarnished by someone else's story about you," she said.

"No. I would not." His entire demeanor changed, and for a moment it was as if Janice was looking at a completely different man. His brows furrowed, and concern registered in his eyes.

Just as quickly, the mischievous smile reappeared. "I'm a reporter, Ms. Eastman. Surely you know that I have to tell the stories as I find them."

"You could use some discretion."

"The *Times* offers a fair report on all stories. Except our opinion column, of course."

"I see. Well, perhaps I could encourage you to play fair as you write any future articles. That last piece nearly did our poor Winnie in."

Oh brother. Why had she said that? The man reached for his pen and scribbled something down on a pad of paper.

A pink pad of paper.

Janice felt as if her heart sailed into her throat as she gazed at the familiar notepad. Her heart thumped so loudly, she wondered if her friends could hear it.

"Whether you like it or not, those messages in the loaves of bread gave me plenty of fodder for stories. Now, I'm sorry that it all happened at your inn, but I can't control that, can I?" Hank gazed at Janice with such intensity, she felt beads of sweat begin to trickle down her back.

On the other hand, it was awfully hot in here. How did the man work under such stifling conditions?

"I'm a reporter. I get to the bottom of things. And in this case, Winnie Washington seems to be standing smack-dab in the center of this story. So, I won't stop until I figure out how and why she put those messages into the loaves of bread. She must have some ulterior motive, wouldn't you say?"

"You can't mean that." Tess put her hands against the edge of his desk and pushed herself to a standing position. "Tell me I did not just hear you suggest that Winnie did this."

He shrugged. "She's the logical choice. What other conclusion could I draw?"

"We won't even entertain that notion." LuAnn waved her hand. "Why would she deliberately do something that could potentially damage her own reputation? Or the inn's? That's ludicrous."

"Right?" Tess plopped back down into her chair.

"I see political parties do it all the time. They drum up negative stories and then accuse their opponent of having done the deed. All to get attention and sympathy. But there's always a reason. Always a motive. We just need to dig a little deeper to find it."

"Winnie needs neither attention nor sympathy." Janice's gaze shifted to a machine in the corner of the room. "And dig all you like—you won't find any dirt on her. She's an amazing woman with a big following. People come from all over to eat her food. So I say we stop this conversation right now before I get any more worked up."

Hank's gaze traveled from Janice to Tess to LuAnn, then back to Janice once again. "Look. I have work to do. Big stories are brewing, even now, and I don't want to miss a thing. I will leave you with these parting words: 'Look no further than your own house for answers.' I believe you will find them there, in abundance." He pushed back his chair and stood. "Now, if you don't mind, I have work to do."

Seconds later, Janice and the others were in the lobby. They found Georgia and Kip sitting side-by-side in a couple of chairs, holding hands.

"What did you find out?" Kip stood and let go of Georgia's hand.

"Nothing much," Janice admitted.

"I'd say it was a complete waste of time." Tess shrugged. "Now what?"

"Now, we keep going," Janice said. "We figure out who put the slips of paper in the bread before he does. Otherwise he'll turn the whole story into a circus."

"Too late." LuAnn shrugged. "Just call me a tightrope walker."

"I want to be the ringmaster," Tess said, and grinned.

"I guess that would make me the clown." Janice sighed. Unfortunately, she couldn't help feeling that Hank Clive already saw them as buffoons, anyway. "Did either of you happen to notice the laminating machine in the corner of his office?"

Tess shook her head. "I was too distracted by the mess to notice anything in particular. I don't think I've ever seen an office in such disarray."

"Me neither. But I did notice the laminating machine. It's an older model. And I also noticed he's got a pad of paper from the competition."

"Free paper?" Georgia suggested. "Anyone could grab one."

"Maybe," Janice said. "But I happened to notice that Hank also had a perfectly good pad of paper sitting next to it in a lovely shade of gray. And if you recall, every time we see him, he's writing on a gray notepad, not a pink one. So, why pick up a pad of the pink at the competition? I find the whole thing rather suspicious."

In fact, Janice found a lot about Hank Clive suspicious. But she wouldn't voice all of her concerns just yet. She still had a bit more research to do on the man before she could point any fingers.

"Here we are, caught up in another mystery." Tess laughed. "We're like a magnet for unsolved stories."

"Hey, we have to live up to our motto, right? 'We will never be boring or bored and we will never act our age.'" LuAnn grinned. "I just got a letter from my cousin in Maryland. Sounds like the biggest goings-on in her life are the shows she watches on television."

"Sad." Janice thought about it for a moment. "I made up my mind years ago that I would stay as active as possible in my golden years. Of course, I didn't realize that would mean tip-toeing downstairs at midnight and lurking at back doors to spy on private conversations. But I love my life—our life—here at Wayfarers. It's crazy to think that God knew, even when I was a young mom—that I would eventually end up here."

"If He knows what's coming—and He does—then He also has to know who put those messages in Winnie's bread. I say we stop right here and now and pray." Tess gestured for the ladies to huddle up. "We'll ask Him to reveal the who, what, when, where, and why to us."

Janice nodded. "Sounds good. And by the way, I'm learning to love that scripture in First Corinthians where God says that He will bring to light the things that are hidden in darkness."

"I wish I had X-ray vision like God does," LuAnn said.

Kip nodded. "Me too. When I was a kid, I always wished for X-ray vision."

LuAnn laughed. "Now I can't even find my sunglasses when they've gone missing."

Tess led the group in prayer, asking the Lord to reveal the truth to them.

Afterward, Janice felt much better about the situation. No matter who had done this, no matter the reasoning behind it, they would get to the bottom of it, with God's help.

Janice glanced at Georgia, who was so busy staring into Kip's eyes that she didn't seem to notice anything or anyone else.

Janice tapped Kip on the shoulder. "Pardon the interruption, but can I ask a question?"

"Hmm?" He looked away from Georgia and glanced Janice's way. "What's that?"

"Why did you take in the puppy? I understand that you have a soft heart and he's a sweet pup and all, but what was really behind your decision?"

Kip didn't say anything at first. After a few moments, the edges of his lips curled up in a smile. "He's a cute little guy, and I couldn't stand the idea of taking him to the pound. And I could tell Georgia liked him too. I was thinking maybe the dog would give me an excuse to see her more." The smile broadened, and a sparkle lit his eyes.

"Mm-hmm." Just as Janice suspected.

Kip shrugged. "Let's just say I have a growing affection for dogs."

He had a growing affection, all right, but she suspected it had little to do with the pup, cute as he was.

"The little guy is growing on me," Kip added. "Almost wish I could keep him."

"Right." Janice turned her attention to Georgia. "Your turn. Just one little question for you."

"What's that, Janice?" Georgia asked, never taking her gaze off Kip.

"You've been sneaking off a lot, which has raised more than a few suspicions. Anything you'd like to say about that?"

Georgia's cheeks flamed pink. "Oh, I..." She released a little giggle.

"It's my fault." Kip raised his hand. "I'm the one who's been distracting her."

"Mm-hmm." Georgia nodded and gazed at him with tenderness. "It's totally his fault."

"Oh, I see," Janice responded. And in that moment, she truly did.

Chapter Twenty-Three

August 20, 1860

Prudence stood along the river's edge and gazed out at the waters where the two rivers met. She allowed her thoughts to travel to the lovely scene, and sighed deeply. In so many ways, the growing troubles between the North and the South reminded her of those two rivers, one and the same, and yet steeply divided. Oh, but the place where they merged together—it was lovely to gaze upon.

If only the disagreements and struggles brewing between the two sides could be remedied as easily as two rivers merging together. Wouldn't it be an inspiring thing, to watch one-time enemies link arms and work together, a mighty force creating a current of love and brotherhood? Such ideas seemed lofty and out of reach at the moment.

Her thoughts shifted to the young woman in Pittsburgh. Was she, like this river, yearning to link heart and arms with her beau from the South? How sad, to think of all the things that stood between them.

She stopped and whispered a prayer, that the treasure she had baked into a fresh loaf of bread had reached its destination by now. Maybe she would never know for sure, but in her heart, Prudence had to believe that love would find a way.

After spending some time in prayer, she made her way home. She went straight to the kitchen to prepare supper. A few minutes later, Jason entered the room with Moses in his arms. He walked over to her and kissed her forehead.

"We got a letter from William. He's made it back to Lexington."

"Praise be." Prudence clasped her hands together. "Such happy news."

"I am still amazed that a man would go to such lengths for his friend."

"He loves Theodore. Like a brother, he said."

"Like that verse thee is always quoting."

"Which one is that?"

"*Greater love hath no man than this, that a man lay down his life for his friends.*' Sounds like William was willing to do that very thing for his friend."

"And what of the woman in Pittsburgh?" Prudence asked. "Has love saved her as well?"

"We are but the messengers, sweet Pru. Only time will tell."

CHAPTER TWENTY-FOUR

When they arrived back at the inn, Winnie was flying around the kitchen, pie paraphernalia strewn on every flat surface. She seemed to be falling apart at the seams. Instead of resting up for the next day's competition, she insisted on plowing through with her recipes. Despite everyone's best attempts to get her out of the kitchen, she would not be deterred.

By early afternoon, she appeared so exhausted she could barely function. Janice found her slumped over the kitchen table with a cold cup of coffee next to her. Had Winnie fallen asleep on the job?

"Good afternoon, sunshine," Janice called out. "Are you in there?"

Winnie groaned but did not lift her head.

Compassion flooded over Janice as she said, "Go home and rest, Winnie. Please. You can't go on like this."

"I don't think I could sleep, even if I went home," Winnie responded, her voice muffled as she remained facedown. "I went to bed at a decent hour but couldn't fall asleep until almost five this morning. When I finally did fall asleep, I had the worst dream ever."

"I'm sorry to hear that. What happened in the dream?"

"I dreamed it was the day of the finals, and someone swapped out my sweet ingredients for savory. For some weird reason, I was stuck with salmon and capers."

"Ick."

"That's what I said. I was so angry, but what choice did I have? I had to bake a savory pie."

Tess entered the room and walked to the coffeepot.

"Did you win?" Janice asked.

Winnie shrugged. "I don't know. I woke up before the end."

"I hate it when that happens." Tess walked their way with the cup of coffee in her hand.

"You hate it when your pie ingredients are stolen?" Winnie asked, still sounding half asleep.

"No, I hate it when a dream gets interrupted, especially when it's a lovely dream."

"Well, this was more of a nightmare, let me tell you." Winnie tried to stand but collapsed back into the chair once again.

Tess clucked her tongue. "There's no easy way to say this, Winnie—you're killing yourself. And it has to end."

Winnie released a quiet groan.

"Yes, Tess is right." Janice pulled up a chair next to her friend and rested a hand on her shoulder. "This is all too much pressure. I'm sorry we ever put that sign up in the first place or made you feel like you had to help us with our marketing plan."

"Agreed," Tess said. "I'll pull that stupid banner down right now if you like."

"No." Winnie's eyes widened. "I don't want people to think I've cracked like an egg. I'll be okay. Just let me get my bearings."

She took a couple of deep breaths and then leaned over to rest her elbows on her knees. "Nothing a little prayer won't fix."

"And sleep," Tess added. "Face it, Winnie. You need sleep."

"I do." Winnie sighed, and her shoulders slumped forward.

"Great idea," Janice agreed. "I say we pray right here, right now, then send you home for the day, Winnie." She stretched out her hand and rested it on Winnie's shoulder and ushered up a quiet prayer.

Georgia came in and tied an apron on just as Janice was a line or two into the prayer. "What's this, a church service?" she asked.

"More like an impromptu prayer meeting," Janice explained. "Feel free to join us."

Georgia still looked a bit taken aback. "At least we're not in the lobby of the newspaper this time. But I'd rather not, thanks."

"Fine, don't pray for me," Winnie muttered. "Never mind the fact that I pray for you every night of my life, Georgia-girl."

"Wait, you pray for me, Winnie?" Georgia looked shocked by this idea.

"Well, sure. I added you to my list the day you came to work for us."

"Well, I guess I could pray for you, then." Georgia slipped into the circle. "As long as I don't have to do it out loud or anything."

A couple of minutes later, LuAnn entered the kitchen, followed by Robin. Before long, they had a regular prayer meeting going.

Afterward, Winnie wore a smile of appreciation. "Thanks for that. I think I've got my energy back."

"I'd still rather you went home to sleep," Janice said.

"Yeah, we can handle things around here," Tess agreed. "We don't have many guests, anyway. We've planned on a continental breakfast for them in the morning."

"I wanted to try out one more recipe." Winnie yawned. "I've come to a final decision about what pie I'm making for the big competition."

"Oh?" Janice paused and leaned against the edge of the counter. "What flavor? Please say chocolate."

"Key lime."

"Well, that's good too. But you know me, I love chocolate."

"I feel like everyone's going to do chocolate, though." Winnie yawned again. "I did give thought to a chocolate hazelnut or maybe a mocha chocolate, but I don't trust myself well enough to try something too out of the box. This is the time to stick to what I know. And I know key lime. It's fruity and fun."

"Just like all of us." LuAnn smiled. "And you could do key lime in your sleep."

"Looks like she's about to." Georgia reached out to steady Winnie, who looked like she might just crumple to the floor.

"No, I'm fine. Really." Winnie put her hand up, as if praising the Lord. "That prayer time will see me through."

Georgia tightened her apron strings and reached for a mixing bowl. "Did you settle on which breads you're doing, Winnie?"

"Mm-hmm. I'll do my mama's Parker House rolls, I think, and maybe some sort of a sweet bread too."

"Cinnamon rolls!" Janice and Tess spoke in unison.

"Yes, you've got to do your cinnamon rolls, Winnie," LuAnn agreed. "I've never had anything like them. They're absolutely yummy."

"Good enough for first place?" Winnie asked.

"We don't care if you place at all, Winnie." Georgia threw her arms around her mentor and held her in a tight hug. "We're just so proud of you. And don't worry about the things that could go wrong. You'll get through it."

"People usually excel under pressure," LuAnn said.

"True." Tess nodded. "Did you know that Jim Thorpe—the Olympic runner—had his shoes stolen on the day of the big race? He dug through the trash and found two shoes that didn't match. One was too big and the other was too small. He wore an extra sock on the foot with the too-big shoe and went on to win the race."

"No excuses for me, I guess." Winnie laughed. "But if anyone thinks they're going to steal anything from me between now and the big day, they'd better think again. I'll be sleeping with one eye open."

This somehow led to a conversation about how Robin had walked in on Reena in the parlor, sleeping with her eyes half-open. Robin shuddered. "But, if we're being honest, that woman makes me nervous, even with her eyes wide open."

"How so?" Janice asked.

Robin shrugged. "I can't put my finger on it, but I'm suspicious of the way she always seems to be snooping around."

Janice had to agree that something about Reena seemed a bit off-kilter. But there were few clues to lead one to a logical conclusion unless you counted the cookie crumbs leading to her bedroom.

Before she left the kitchen, Janice turned her attention to Robin to ask a question. "Robin, have you seen the laminating machine in the office?"

"Which machine is that?"

"It's small and black and sits in the far corner on a little end table."

"Oh, right. Yes, I've seen it. I noticed it when I was in there a week or so ago, cleaning up."

"Was it dusty?"

"Was it ever!" Robin laughed. "You know, for a place that prides itself on cleanliness, we sure let that office get out of sorts. But don't worry, Janice. I gave it a thorough cleaning."

"You're saying you cleaned the laminating machine?

"Of course. I couldn't leave it like that." Her brows knit. "Did I do something wrong?"

"No, honey. Of course not. Thank you for being so thorough."

"Oh, good. I was afraid I'd upset you somehow. Seems like a lot of folks around here are hot and bothered lately. The last thing I want to do is get anyone else riled up."

This certainly got Janice's attention. "Who's hot and bothered?"

"Oh, you know…Mrs. Newberry. She was in the library muttering something under her breath about how we don't pay enough attention to her—about how we invited her to come and stay but then ignored her. I couldn't make any sense out of it."

"Invited her to come and stay?" Janice had to wonder again if the poor old woman was suffering from dementia. "None of us have any idea what she's doing here."

"To hear her talk, you'd think she was an invited guest." Robin chuckled. "But then again, what do I know? I'm just the hired help." She grinned and tiptoed out of the kitchen.

Janice decided to pay Reena a visit. True to Robin's words, she found the woman dozing in a chair in the library area. Janice cleared her throat as she entered the room, and Reena stirred.

"Oh, there you are."

"Yes, here I am." Janice smiled.

"I was starting to think you ladies had forgotten all about me."

"Now, how could we ever forget you, Reena?"

She shrugged and adjusted her position in the chair. As she did, a pink notepad fell to the floor. Janice leaned down to pick it up and noticed the top page was covered in handwriting. She passed the notepad back to Reena, who clutched it like a prized possession.

"Do you mind if I ask you a question, Reena?" Janice said after a moment of silence.

"Of course not. What is it?"

"Where did you get that tablet?"

Reena's cheeks blazed pink. "Oh, I suppose there's no point in lying about it. I took it from the kitchen a while back. I needed something to write on."

"But why take it?" Janice asked. "You could have asked me for one. I have dozens of notepads."

"I probably should have. But the truth of the matter is, I didn't want anyone to know what I was up to. If I'd asked for a notepad, you might have wondered what I needed it for."

"True. I might have."

Reena's eyes sparkled. "I suppose at my age there's no point in keeping secrets. I've been making diary entries, much like my great-great-grandmother did, and I ran out of paper. I thought the pink was just perfect. I saw it in the kitchen when I snuck in there to steal a cookie from the cookie jar." She put her finger to her lips. "Shh! Don't tell Winnie, okay? I certainly don't want her to know I snuck into her kitchen."

"We have more than one cookie lover around here." Janice laughed. "But what were you saying about your great-great-grandmother? She kept a diary?"

Reena nodded. "Nothing unusual about that, I suppose. Most folks did, back in those days. But my goodness, did she ever have some stories to tell. I daresay you couldn't write a modern romance novel that would surpass the one she almost had."

"Almost had?" Janice echoed.

Reena nodded, and a hint of pain filled her eyes. "She came so close, you see. So very close."

Janice swallowed hard as hope settled over her like a warm blanket on a cool day. Was this the same great-great-grandmother she and Tess and LuAnn had read about? Was there really a way to find out more of her story? "What was her name, Reena?" she asked after a moment of silence.

"Her name?" Reena looked puzzled. "Why, Birdie Atkinson, of course. But I seem to recall you already knew that when you sent the invitation for me to come to Wayfarers Inn in the first place."

CHAPTER TWENTY-FIVE

Sent the invitation for you to come to Wayfarers Inn?" Now
Janice was truly puzzled. "What do you mean?"

Reena adjusted her position in the chair. "Such a strange
letter to receive, but I came at your invitation, of course. And
I've spent days trying to figure out why you wanted me here.
I've sat at that café table waiting for someone to fill me in or
give me some sort of clue. I've dozed off in this very chair more
times than I can count, waiting for someone to approach me
with the reason behind it all. But, as of yet, I cannot ascertain
why my presence was requested. I thought this might be some
game you were playing with me, but if it is, I don't care for it at
all. There's nothing worse than coming such a distance, only to
be ignored altogether."

"I'm sorry." Janice paced the room then turned to look at
the elderly woman. "This is all so perplexing. To my knowledge, no one from the inn sent an invitation."

"You didn't?" Reena's smile faded. "You didn't want me?"

"It's not like that, Reena. We simply didn't know you. Had
we known you…" She paused, not knowing how to finish the
sentence.

"This is such an odd revelation. I received a handwritten letter two weeks ago, asking me to come to Wayfarers

Inn and stay if I wanted to learn more about my family's history."

"Your family's history?"

"Of course. Why else did you think I would stay so long?"

Janice knelt down beside her chair and patted her hand. "I would definitely remember sending a handwritten letter," she said. "It's been a long time since I wrote one of those."

Tess and LuAnn came into the room and saw Janice kneeling next to Reena. They must have assumed the worst, because Tess came rushing their way. "Is everything okay?"

"Something rather troubling has happened," Reena said. "And neither of us can make sense of it."

Janice quickly relayed the story, and LuAnn's eyes widened. "Wow. So someone sent you a invitation to come to the inn. But why? And which side of your family are you interested in learning more about, Reena?"

"My great-great-grandmother's. Birdie Atkinson. It's the rest of her story I've come all this way to discover. Please don't make me wait any longer. This whole journey has been arduous enough, don't you think?"

"Birdie Atkinson." LuAnn shook her head. "So we were right? She's the one in Prudence's journal?"

"Yes," Janice responded. "Birdie from Pittsburgh. And something about a treasure."

"Yes, that's right!" Reena grinned. "A gold ring! It's in my room at this very moment. That's how I knew Wayfarers Inn was part of my story. You mentioned the ring in the invitation. It was so sweet of you to do that."

Janice's heart skipped a beat. The ring that had tumbled onto the floor that day in Reena's room…was the treasure that Prudence had baked into a loaf of bread one and a half centuries ago? "The letter you received mentioned the ring?" she asked.

"Well, of course. You asked me to bring it, remember? I've been keeping it safe in my room, thinking you would ask about it at any time."

Tess bolted out of the room and returned moments later, diary in hand.

"Start at the beginning, Reena," she implored. "Please. I need to compare stories."

"From what I've read in Birdie's diary," Reena said, "she first visited extended family in Lexington, Kentucky, as a youngster. This was years before the war, when it was still safe to travel back and forth from Pennsylvania to Kentucky. She and her family made the journey every year, according to my research, anyway. From what I've gathered—and I've done quite a bit of research on the matter—she fell in love with a neighbor of theirs, a young man named Theodore."

"The man in Prudence's diary was name William," Janice said. "I wonder how he knew Theodore and why he had the ring."

Reena looked perplexed by this comment. "You keep mentioning a Prudence. Who is she?"

"I suppose it makes sense that you wouldn't know Prudence's name, since Birdie never met her." Tess held out the diary and promised to read the story aloud once Reena finished her part of the tale.

"My grandmother's story didn't end well, I'm afraid." Reena released a sigh. "You see, she turned eighteen in the summer of 1860, and Theodore asked her to marry him. She returned to Pittsburgh with her family. Her beau was not free to come to her for some reason, and of course she was not free to go to him."

"Those were troubled times, to be sure, right before the war broke out." Tess set Prudence's diary down on the end table.

"Yes. But there's a story—and I've heard it from relatives on both her maternal and paternal sides—that somehow he got a ring to her and asked her to wait for him to come. It is the same ring that I now possess."

Janice squeezed Reena's hand. "We think we know how he got the ring to Birdie, Reena. Prudence was a woman who worked at this inn when it was the Riverfront House. In August of 1860 a young man named William came to the inn with a 'treasure' that he had to get from Lexington to Pittsburgh. Prudence hid the treasure in a loaf of bread so anyone who tried to rob him on the road wouldn't find it."

"This William must have been a friend of Theodore's," Reena said. "But even though the ring was delivered, she couldn't marry Theodore. Her father would not allow it. And she could not travel back to Kentucky in defiance of her father, because it was too dangerous. Her father arranged a marriage with a well-to-do banker who lived in Pittsburgh. She married him against her own wishes." Reena paused, and tears brimmed her lashes. "That's why I relate to her, I suppose. Her story is very much my own. Not the part about the ring in the bread, though."

"And now we are seeing a story play out with eerie similarities." Janice rose and paced the room. "This can't be a coincidence. Someone who knows about the love story between Birdie and Theodore put messages in Winnie's bread loaves. And whoever did this also knows enough to involve you, Reena." She turned to face the elderly woman. "We didn't send that invitation. Someone else did. And I suspect that someone else has been in and out of this inn over the past few days, watching our every move."

"But, who?" said Tess. "And why?"

"I don't know, but I've got the shivers just thinking about it." LuAnn held out her arm. "Look at that. The hairs on my arm are standing up."

"Mine too." Tess picked up Prudence's diary and held it close. "This story gets stranger and stranger."

"One thing I can say for sure. William sounds like a man who was willing to lay down his life for a friend. He certainly went the extra mile to ensure Theodore's happiness." Janice paused and then said, "Oh my."

"What is it, Janice?" Tess asked.

"I've just described Winnie. She's gone above and beyond to help us, just like William did for Theodore. She's worked round the clock to make sure we were all happy, that the inn was well represented, even to her own detriment."

"Well, when you put it like that..." Tess pursed her lips.

Janice's gaze shifted to Reena. "I have a question for you," she said. "You've been with us for days now. How long would you have waited for one of us to say something about all of this?"

"I was getting close to giving up," she said. She paused, and her eyes brimmed with tears once again. Reena's head drooped forward. "I can't make anyone understand what it's like to be forced to marry someone you don't really love."

Whoa. Well, that certainly got Janice's attention. "What do you mean?" she asked after a moment of careful reflection.

Reena paused, her gaze still shifted downward. "I come from a family where prestige and money mean a lot. Those things often stand in the way of you marrying whomever you choose. My father was the sort to look for a good match for me, and he thought he'd found it in James O'Brien."

"Wait...O'Brien?" Now Janice was really confused.

"Yes. We were married for forty-three years. When he passed away five years ago, I took back my maiden name. I wanted to go back to who I was all those years ago, when the world was my oyster."

"I can't believe your father married you off like that," LuAnn said. "I thought the days of matchmaking were long behind us."

"It probably wasn't as severe as I'm making it sound. My father had his point of view about what made for a stable marriage, and I had a different one. But I wasn't the type to stand up to people, so I went along with his way of thinking in the end. And please don't misunderstand me. The marriage wasn't all bad. We had good times and bad, like all couples. I had a very cordial relationship with my husband, though my dream of having children never came to pass. What a disappointment I was to him in that regard." Reena released a sigh and seemed to lose herself to her thoughts.

"I'm sorry, Reena." Janice rested her hand on the woman's shoulder.

"Please don't be. We never shared the kind of love that most girls hope to have, but we had a marriage in name, which gave me a certain place among the people we knew." She shrugged. "Not that a place in society can fill the void in a broken heart. I spent my whole marriage focusing on what might have been if I'd had the courage to choose what I really wanted. That's why I related to Birdie on such a deep level. When I found her diary, when I read that she had lived through a similar circumstance, I just had to get to know her better."

"Wow." Janice paused to think through Reena's words. She and Lawrence had been fortunate. Their relationship—though frazzled at times, due to his heavy workload at the church—was based on a deep, abiding love for each other. How terrible, to have to commit your life to someone you didn't really love. How sad, for both parties.

The ladies spent a full hour reading entries from the two diaries to each other. Reena wept when she heard Prudence's words about William, knowing what he did because of his devotion to his friend. And Janice found herself tearing up as she heard Birdie's words of affection for Theodore, the man she truly loved. What a twisted tale of love won and lost.

As they wrapped up their time together, Tess closed Prudence's diary. "We've learned a lot about the past," she said. "But not as much about the present-day story. We still have no idea who put the messages in the loaves of bread . . . or how they got them there."

"I say we worry about that after tomorrow's competition," Janice suggested. "From now until then, let's focus all of our attention on Winnie. She deserves that from us."

"Yes, but I'll be focusing from my bed," Reena said. "It's three o'clock. Time for an afternoon nap, if you don't mind."

"Of course not." Janice extended her hand to help Reena up from the chair, then all of the women took the elevator up to the third floor to make sure their guest made it to her room okay. Before she headed off down the hallway, Reena looked back at them and waved.

"Thank you, ladies," she said with a wink. "I have a feeling we're all going to be great friends."

"You're a wise woman, Reena Newberry," Janice responded. "A wise woman indeed."

Reena pointed to her face and said, "I am more than the sum of my wrinkles." A sly smile tipped up the edges of her lips. "Though, frankly, with as many wrinkles as I have, that'd be quite a sum. Not sure I can count that high."

The Inn Crowd erupted in laughter. LuAnn and Tess were still laughing as they climbed the stairs to the fourth floor. Janice walked down to the lobby, overcome by all she'd learned. To think that Reena had thought for all this time that she'd been invited to come to the inn. How sad and lonely the poor woman must have felt—thinking she'd been invited but then rarely spoken to. Janice made up her mind to give this precious woman a place of honor in the inn for as long as she cared to stay. Anyone who had loved and lost as much as Reena had certainly deserved the care of those around her.

As she made her way toward the parlor, Janice couldn't still her mind. What amazing revelations this day had brought.

One troubling thought remained, however. Someone was still out there, sabotaging the inn, someone with a connection to both Reena and the Inn Crowd. The list had narrowed over the past few hours, and the suspects who remained were fresh in Janice's mind.

CHAPTER TWENTY-SIX

Early that evening Janice suggested they make a quick run to get ice cream. She even managed to talk Reena, Winnie, and Georgia into coming with them. Reena couldn't contain her joy at being included. She didn't even grumble when Kip joined them with the hyper chiweenie.

They had a marvelous time walking to Fundae. Once they settled down at one of the outdoor tables, each with his or her favorite creamy delight, Janice felt overwhelmed with joy. She looked around the table and took in each wonderful face—LuAnn, with her double-dip Rocky Road, Tess, with her single scoop sweet cream, Georgia and Kip, who had decided to share a hot fudge sundae, Winnie, with a strawberry shake, and Reena, with a mini cup of mint chocolate chip ice cream. Each person represented at the table was as unique as the flavors of ice cream, and Janice wouldn't trade any one of them in. Even Dobbins seemed to be enjoying his pupsicle as he lounged at their feet.

After they finished their ice cream, Janice encouraged everyone to continue their walk. She had an ulterior motive but did not voice it aloud. They made their way down the sidewalk, finally passing in front of the Better Batter, where she came to a grinding halt. It was a summer Friday night, and the shop was still open for another thirty minutes.

Winnie stood and gazed upward at the sign above the store. "Seems pretty cute," she said after a moment of quiet reflection. "I wonder what it looks like inside."

"Oh, it's adorable," Tess said. "We were here last week and bought a few sweet treats."

"You were?" Winnie looked her way. "Cupcakes, perhaps? In a really cute box that ended up in my kitchen trash can?"

"Oh, right." Tess's expression shifted to one of concern. "I forgot you found out about that."

Winnie waved her hand and appeared to dismiss any concerns. "No, it's okay. Shop where you like. Eat what you like." She continued to look over the storefront. "Like I said, it looks really cute. I can see the draw."

"You want to go inside?" Janice asked. "It's the only way to see for yourself what she's up to in there."

"Sure. I'd like that."

"I'll stay out here with Dobbins," Kip said. "We'll be right over here, taking a little siesta." He pointed to an empty bench nearby.

Georgia gave him a little peck on the cheek, and his face flushed.

As they pulled back the door to walk inside, a little bell jingled. Music came from the speakers overhead. Janice smiled when she recognized the tune. The Archies singing "Sugar, Sugar" brought a fun, upbeat rhythm to the room. The edges of Winnie's lips curled up in a smile as she took it all in, followed by a wide-eyed "wow" when she laid eyes on the bakery cases, loaded to the brim with beautifully decorated cakes, cupcakes, cookies, and breads.

"This reminds me of a sweet little bakery I used to visit in Pittsburgh." Reena rushed to the cookie case and pointed to the second shelf. "Would you look at that! Oatmeal raisin. They're my favorite! Ooh, and I love peanut butter." She pointed to the top row. "Those look dreamy. It all looks so inviting and yummy."

Winnie walked from case to case, *oohing* and *aahing*. "I've never seen this much stuff all in one place before. She must bake 24/7." She stopped in front of the bread case.

"Hey, check that out," Georgia said. "Her bread looks just like yours, Winnie."

"Sure does. If I didn't know any different, I'd say it was mine." Winnie leaned down to have a closer look. "She must use the same loaf pan. Once you find a good one, you never go back."

A cheerful voice sounded from behind one of the cases on the far side of the room. "Hello! Welcome to the Better Batter. So glad to see you again." Sandie headed toward them, arms open wide. She gave each person a hug, then her brows knitted together in a pained expression. "I owe you a huge apology."

"Why is that?" Janice asked.

The lines of concentration deepened around Sandie's eyes. "The last time you came into the shop, I was in a terrible mood."

"I must confess, I thought you were a little put off by us," Tess said. "I thought maybe it was something we said...or did."

Sandie shook her head. "Nothing could be further from the truth. It had absolutely nothing to do with you. I was just dealing with a huge fiasco. One of my suppliers messed up an order. Instead of sending me eighty pounds of granulated sugar, they sent eighty pounds of raw sugar. Now I ask you, what would I do with eighty pounds of raw sugar?"

"Oh my." Winnie's eyes widened. "I hope they did right by you."

"In the end, yes, but it took several phone calls to get it straightened out. And, of course, they had to adjust my bill. What a pain!"

"I can't even imagine." Winnie shook her head.

"I know. And trust me when I say I'm a real stickler for getting product out on time." She gestured to the glass cases. "I like to put on a show with my sweets."

"I'd say you do an amazing job with that," Janice said. "It's all so eye-catching."

"Thanks." Sandie paused and walked behind one of the cases to straighten a tray that was slightly crooked. "I'm all about doing things in an organized fashion. If I say I'm going to have chocolate pie on Tuesday, I'm going to have chocolate pie on Tuesday. If I say I'll have peanut butter cookies on Thursday, then that's what I'll have. I'd already advertised my upcoming specials, and my supplier didn't seem at all worried that he couldn't get me the sugar in time, so I had to make a quick dash to the store. I'm not used to operating on the fly like that."

"If anything like that ever happens again, just ask me," Winnie said. "I'll be happy to loan you whatever you like. I'll even bring it to you and help you bake it up."

To Janice's surprise, Sandie burst into tears. "You have no idea what that means to me, Winnie. Seriously." She came out from behind the glass case and wrapped her arms around Winnie.

Winnie's eyes flooded with tears. She patted Sandie on the back and let her cry it out.

After a moment, Sandie stepped back and dried her eyes with the hem of her apron. "I'm just not used to people helping me. I've had to do everything on my own. This is an impossible business to be in, as I'm sure you know, and even harder when you're on your own."

Janice hardly knew what to say in response. She understood, of course, how difficult it was to start up a business. But at least she had the Inn Crowd behind her. She wasn't walking this road alone, as Sandie obviously was.

"And don't even get me started on how tough things were in culinary school." Sandie gestured for the women to sit at a couple of the small café tables. She plopped into a chair next to Winnie and leaned her elbows on the table. "It was a cutthroat environment."

"I can't even imagine," Winnie said.

"I guess that's why I signed up for the Rising Star competition when I first got to town. Maybe I felt like I needed to prove something—to myself, to my parents—who, by the way, always told me I'd made a mistake by thinking I could open my own shop." She broke down in tears once again.

"You poor, sweet girl." These words came from Reena, who appeared to be taking Sandie's meltdown to heart.

Winnie seemed to be taking Sandie's story hard too. She slipped her arm over the young woman's shoulders and held her close.

"I'm so sorry you haven't had the support system you've needed, Sandie," Winnie said. "Sometimes I feel like I don't know what I did to deserve the women God has surrounded me with."

"Can I borrow your women?" A hint of a smile tipped up the corners of Sandie's lips. "I'm only partly kidding."

Winnie gave Tess, Janice, and LuAnn each a look of admiration and love. "We all need a support team, and these ladies are the best in town. I'll be happy to farm them out. If you're ever in need of an encouraging word—"

"Or someone to sample your wares…" Reena added. She licked her lips in an exaggerated fashion.

This got a laugh out of everyone at the table, especially Georgia.

"Just ask," Winnie said. "That's the thing about these ladies. We're family."

"I'm sure that must feel wonderful." Sandie sighed and gazed down at the table. "I haven't had that in a really long time. In fact, I'm not sure I ever had it. I was an only child growing up, and my parents were both workaholics. They shuffled me off to this babysitter or that babysitter, and I didn't have much of a social life. No real friends my own age. But one of my sitters—Mrs. Goddard—taught me to bake." Sandie's frown became a smile. "God bless that woman. She really gave me incentive to go into that big empty kitchen and turn nothing into something. What an amazing teacher she was."

"Maybe you could pick up where she left off. You could teach baking classes to kids at your shop." The suggestion came from Georgia. "I would have loved an opportunity like that as a kid. And I know my parents would've paid for it."

"You think?" Sandie chewed her lip.

"Of course. That's it. Perfect idea!" Winnie practically squealed. "You're young and fun and have such a cute shop. It's perfect for that sort of thing. Get the kids in there and teach them how to roll out pie dough or cut out sugar cookies. You could even show them how to make royal icing and decorate. They'd love that."

"Perfect idea for the holidays too," Janice said. "In fact, you could open it up to families. Parents and kids love to bake together during the Christmas season anyway, but most moms aren't really sure how to make their cookies look very professional."

"My mind is reeling." Sandie smiled. "Thank you. And thanks again for overlooking how grumpy I was the last time you stopped by." She looked at Georgia. "I'm afraid I was a little rude when I saw you at the exhibit the other day as well. I was so embarrassed that I'd asked you to come work for me. I really wasn't trying to steal you away from the inn. I just really, really needed—need—the help." She gestured to the shop. "I'm here day and night. I keep the craziest hours."

"If I lived in Marietta permanently, I could help out." Georgia shrugged. "I'd love to go back and forth between the inn and the bakery, especially if you're going to start teaching classes. Kind of a shame my college is so far away."

"Well, you need to do what's best for you," Sandie responded. "That's a lesson I had to learn the hard way. I had very little encouragement to follow my dream, as I said. And then, things just went from bad to worse."

"How so?" Georgia asked.

Janice braced herself. She, Tess, and LuAnn had done their research. They knew Sandie's story, at least part of it.

"The past five years have been the hardest of my life." Sandie's eyes brimmed with tears once more. "My parents were both killed in a car accident when I was a sophomore in college."

"Oh, Sandie!" Georgia rose and walked over to her, then gave her a big hug. "I'm so sorry. I can't even imagine."

"As I mentioned, we weren't that close. But when I lost them both at the same time, it was almost too much to bear. Mrs. Goddard, God bless her, was a saving grace in my life. But she passed away six months ago from pancreatic cancer. It was horrible."

"This is all so awful." Georgia sat back down, looking completely defeated.

"I don't mind saying it changed everything for me. I couldn't even force myself to get out of bed."

"I know what that feels like," Janice admitted. "I was the same after my husband died."

"I've been through seasons like that too," Winnie admitted. "But baking always puts me in a happy frame of mind."

"Same here." Sandie reached over and squeezed Winnie's hand. "The one thing that brought me comfort was baking. Even on days when I couldn't muster up the strength to get dressed, I would still find myself in the kitchen baking—sugar cookies, cakes, pies, you name it. I just love the process of creating. It brought comfort. So, after a while, I realized this might be the answer, something to pull me out of the pit, so to speak. I signed up for culinary school and next thing you know, I'm up to my elbows in pastry dough and cake batter."

"Wow." Winnie gave her a look of admiration. "You really picked yourself up by your bootstraps. I'm so proud of you, Sandie."

Sandie squeezed Winnie's hand. "Thank you. I don't know that anyone has ever said that to me before, Winnie."

"Are you serious?"

Sandie nodded.

Janice felt a lump grow in her throat as she watched all of this. Sandie certainly didn't seem to be the sort to sabotage the inn, not now, anyway. But there was still one lingering question, one question that needed to be answered.

"Sandie..." Janice turned to face her. "Do you sell a lot of bread?"

Sandie's face lit in a smile. "Yes. You ladies wouldn't believe how much bread I baked in the first few days after the competition. All sorts of folks came through wanting it. One lovely benefit of doing well at the competition, I guess."

"Glad to know I wasn't the only one sweating over a hot oven." Winnie smiled and released her hold on Sandie's hand.

"I was sweating, all right. One night I stayed at the bakery until almost midnight baking loaf after loaf."

Janice frowned, her motherly instincts rising. "I really don't like the idea of you being all alone in the bakery so late."

Sandie shrugged. "It doesn't bother me too much. And I'm not always alone. Hank Clive has stopped by a couple of times."

"Hank Clive?" all of the ladies asked in unison.

"Yes. One night he saw my light on and knocked on the door. I let him in, and he ended up staying for a while to visit. That man really loves my bread." Sandie's lips curled up in a smile. "He's one of my best customers. He makes a lot of purchases for the homeless shelter. I do make a good loaf of bread, if I do say so myself." Her cheeks flushed the prettiest shade of pink.

Winnie gasped. "Is it really seven thirty?" She pointed to the large colorful clock on the far wall. "I've got to get home."

The women rose and said their goodbyes. Sandie followed them to the front door.

When they stepped outside onto the deck, a glorious sunset greeted them. The precocious chiweenie came bounding their way.

"Dobbins! Sweet puppy! I missed y—" Georgia took a step toward the pooch, tripped over him, and went flying across the wooden deck. She hit the ground with a thud.

"Oh, no!" Kip sprang from his spot on the bench and came running toward her.

Janice knelt down beside Georgia. "Are you okay?"

"I...I..." Janice watched in alarm as Georgia tried to move her right arm, but couldn't. "Ugh. My wrist."

"Do you think it's broken?" Tess asked.

"I had a broken wrist once," Reena said. "Couldn't use it for weeks."

Kip helped Georgia stand and led her to the bench. "I'm so sorry. It's all my fault. I fell asleep, and I guess I let go of Dobbins's leash."

Sandie came out of her shop to see what all the commotion was about. She took one look at Georgia and offered to call 911.

"No, please don't do that." Georgia winced. "I'll be okay."

"It might not be bad enough to involve an ambulance, but you're going to let us take you to one of those urgent care clinics, at the very least." Tess flew into action and gave instructions—Winnie and LuAnn would return to the inn with Reena, and she and Janice would take Georgia to the doctor. With Kip's help, of course.

Before they parted ways, Georgia hugged Winnie with her good arm. "I'm so sorry. It doesn't look like I'll be able to assist you at the finals, Winnie."

"Not your fault, honey. You just heal up. Get better. Besides, I'm sure one of these fine ladies will be happy to step into your spot and assist me."

Janice swallowed hard and tried to disappear behind the others. No way would she be comfortable on a stage in front of thousands of people. The TV cameras would add an extra level of intimidation. Judging from the body language coming from Tess and LuAnn, they weren't interested either.

"Well, who's it gonna be?" Winnie looked from person to person.

After a few moments of awkward silence, Sandie said, "What about me?" The edges of her lips curled up in a smile. "I know a little something about baking, and I'd love to help, Winnie. I'm sure Jennie will be happy to cover for me here at the shop."

Janice's gaze traveled back and forth between Sandie and Winnie, anticipation building.

After a moment, Winnie nodded. "That sounds like a fine proposition. And if you're half as good as everyone says you are, we can't lose."

Sandie shrugged. "I don't know about all of that, but I would be honored to join you. I still have so much to learn, and you've been at this for years."

"Is she calling me old?" Winnie put her hands on her hips and then laughed—a loud, comfortable laugh that put everyone at ease.

Just as LuAnn and Winnie turned to head back toward the inn, Kip took several steps in their direction with Dobbins on the leash. He looked back and forth among the women, then thrust the dog's leash into Reena's hands.

"Take care of him for us, will you, Miss Reena? Please?"

For a moment, the poor woman looked as if she might release her hold on the leash. Then, just as quickly, she clucked her tongue and bid the little fellow follow her to the inn.

CHAPTER TWENTY-SEVEN

The morning of the big competition, Janice, Tess, and LuAnn set out muffins and scones and fresh fruit for their guests and then gathered in the lobby to share a cup of coffee before kicking off the big day. They invited Reena to join them. She was happy to be included and settled in like one of the family.

Winnie and Georgia arrived a short while later, Georgia looking a little bedraggled.

"How's the wrist today, sweetie?" Janice asked her. "Still hurting?"

Her face contorted as she reached to touch the sling. "I'm loaded up on meds, but I think I must've slept wrong. It's really aching today."

"I'm so glad it's just a sprain," Tess said. "But in all honesty, sometimes those hurt more than breaks."

Georgia released a loud groan.

"Just rest, hon," LuAnn said.

"I will. But first, coffee." Georgia headed over to the coffee-pot. She tried to fill a cup with her left hand, but was unable to. Janice jumped up to help her.

Robin buzzed into the lobby, a frown on her face. "I hate to be the bearer of bad news, but we just got a call from that reporter. He says he'll be at the finals in Columbus later today so he can capture the story for the *Times*. Don't even ask me what I wanted to say in response." She sighed. "You'll be happy to know I kept my mouth shut."

"That fella—what's his name?—still gives me a bad feeling." Reena took a sip of her coffee. "I don't know why he's such a pest or why he should care so much about what goes on around here."

"You're right about that, Reena. Hank Clive is a pest." Janice did her best not to groan aloud as she thought about seeing him in Columbus at today's event. Couldn't he just leave well enough alone?

Reena set her coffee cup down and stared at Janice. "Did you say Clive?"

"Yes, Hank Clive," Janice repeated.

"Please stop saying that name." Winnie rose and walked to the stove. "If I never hear it again, it'll be just fine with me."

Reena's eyes narrowed. "Why does that name sound so familiar?"

Janice reached over to pat the older woman's hand. "You were here the day he came by to visit with Winnie and get information for his article. That's probably why it's ringing a bell. He's a tough one to forget."

"Oh, yes." But this didn't seem to satisfy Reena. She continued to mutter the word, "Clive. Clive." After going silent for a moment, she snapped to attention. "Yes! I remember now. Theodore Clive was the name of the man who proposed to

Birdie, the one who sent the ring all those years ago. I knew it sounded familiar."

The lobby came alive as all the ladies started talking over one another. In the middle of the chaos, Kip walked in with Dobbins. The dog went straight to Reena, who scooped him up into her arms.

"Reena? Are you sure?" Janice asked.

"Sure about what?" Kip asked. "Hey, you guys got any coffee left?"

Winnie pointed to the coffeepot, and he served himself.

"I don't remember reading anything in either diary that specified Theodore's last name," Tess said.

"Who's Theodore?" Kip asked.

Georgia gestured for him to be quiet.

He took his cup of coffee and walked over to the cookie jar. "Got any more snickerdoodles, Winnie?"

"Oh, for Pete's sake." Winnie sprang from her seat and fetched some cookies from the pantry for him. "Now let us finish this conversation, Kip."

"Okay." He settled down at the table and took a bite of his cookie, then spoke with a full mouth. "Looks like I caught you all in the middle of something."

"That's putting it mildly." Georgia reached to take his hand.

"There's no last name mentioned in the diary that I recall," Reena said. "It was in the invitation, remember?" She paused and then shook her head. "Oh, I remember. You didn't actually send that invitation. Someone else did."

"Right." Tess nodded. "But I say we do some research online and try to search the Clive name to see if there's any relationship between the sender of that ring and the man sitting in the office at the *Marietta Times* right now."

Janice's heart raced with excitement as she realized the magnitude of this discovery. "If so, I'd say we've found our culprit."

"Wait." Kip put his hand up, like a student trying to get the teacher's attention. "You all think Hank Clive had something to do with the messages in the bread?"

"Yes!" they all responded at once.

Kip's eyes widened.

Tess went to fetch her computer. Once she returned, she got online and went straight to her favorite ancestry website.

"Once you locate an individual on here, you can go backward in time to the parents and grandparents and so on," she explained. She pointed at the screen. "See? I've done my family's tree all the way back to the 1700s. I'm sure I can figure out if there's a connection between Hank Clive and Theodore. But let's start with Hank."

It took several minutes of searching, checking, and double- and triple-checking, but soon enough the ladies had their answer. Theodore Clive was Hank's great-great-great-grandfather. Just as the diary said, he lived in Lexington, Kentucky, during the Civil War.

"Wow." Tess leaned back in her chair. "Well, that was worth the effort, wasn't it?"

"Indeed." Reena petted the dog. "So, Hank Clive is—what did you say? A great-great-great-grandson of Theodore Clive?"

"Yes, that's right." Tess nodded.

"And I'm guessing Hank is the one who sent you that invitation," Janice added. "He wanted you here, though I'm not sure why."

"A reason that involved his long-ago relative, that much is for sure." Reena seemed to lose herself to her thoughts for a moment. "I did wonder about the handwriting," she said at last. "More chicken scratch than the sort of handwriting you'd expect in a formal invitation."

"Chicken scratch?" Janice asked.

"Kind of like the notes in the bread?" Tess added.

Reena's eyes widened. "Oh my goodness. I never put that together, but I suppose you're right."

"Can we see the invitation, Reena?" Janice asked.

"Yes, of course. It's in my room. Give me a few minutes, and I'll be right back with it." She rose, and Georgia offered to accompany her to her room. A couple of minutes later the hum of the elevator kicked in.

Tess pushed to her feet and stretched her back. "I'm guessing that invitation is in the same handwriting as the notes in the bread."

Janice nodded. "And I'd be willing to say the whole thing was done by one rather infamous reporter, just to get a story."

"One that involved his own family." Winnie paced the room. "But why? And more importantly, how? If he did it, when did he have access? And how in the world did he manage all of this right under our noses?"

"Wait." Janice put her hand up in the air as a memory struck her. "He purchased bread from Sandie. She told us so herself."

"I thought that homeless shelter story sounded a little too contrived," Winnie said.

Sandie arrived moments later. She took one look at the women and glanced at her watch. "Am I late?"

"No," Janice assured her. "We're just having a cup of coffee before leaving for the competition." She paused. "Sandie, I have a question. You mentioned Hank Clive coming by your shop."

"Yes, he's quite a fan." Sandie took a seat and rested her hands in her lap.

"Right. I'm just wondering, when did he first buy bread from you?"

"Hmm." Sandie paused. "I'm pretty sure he asked for the first dozen loaves the day after the competition. I remember it was a Sunday, because the shop wasn't open, but I went in and baked anyway."

"Wait...a dozen? Who would buy a dozen loaves of bread?" Tess interjected.

"Someone who says he's going to donate them to a homeless shelter." Sandie's face lit in a smile. "He's such a sweetheart, y'all. He came to me right after the bread round to say how much he enjoyed my bread and how he thought I should've won." She giggled. "Oops. Probably shouldn't have told you that part."

"No, I'm glad to have the information," Janice said. "What else did he say?"

"Only that he had done an article on the homeless shelter and knew they were short on food during the summer. Even though it was a lot of work, I was happy to bake for them because I knew it was going to a good cause."

Janice turned her attention to the other ladies in the room. "Do any of you remember an article in the *Times* about the homeless shelter?" She looked from woman to woman. They all shook their heads.

"Not me," Tess said.

"Pretty sure I would have remembered that," LuAnn added.

"I don't remember it either." Janice turned her attention back to Sandie. "Did he show you the article?"

"No. I never thought to ask. Just took him at his word."

"Just took him at his word." Janice sighed.

"I'm on it." Tess went back to work on her laptop. She pulled up the *Marietta Times* website and started searching, looking for anything she could on the homeless shelter. "Last article I see in here was from last Christmas—a plea for folks to donate toys and such. I certainly don't see anything about a food drive this summer."

"Summer would be an odd time for that, anyway," Georgia said. "Don't shelters usually do their food drives around Thanksgiving or Christmas?"

"Homeless people need to eat at other times of the year too," Winnie said. "So anything is possible."

"Right," Sandie said. "But why would Hank lead me to believe the bread was for a *current* food drive if no such drive existed? He specifically said he'd done an article in the *Times* about the drive. Oh, I feel like such a goober. I should have checked."

"There was no reason for you to suspect he wasn't telling the truth," Janice said. "But now that you mention it, I don't recall seeing any advertisements around town for this so-called food drive."

"I say we stop talking about suspects and focus on Winnie," Tess said.

Sandie turned to face her new friend and offered a smile. "Winnie, I'm more excited about riding to Columbus with you and getting to know you than I am about the actual event."

The two women started chatting about their plan of action once they arrived in Columbus, but Janice couldn't focus on their conversation, not with so many troubling thoughts about Hank Clive floating through her mind. If he sabotaged them once, would he do it again—say, at today's event?

Chapter Twenty-Eight

Janice offered to drive the crew to Columbus for the Rising Star finals. Reena stayed behind at the inn with Robin and Thorn, who had returned to finish up his work on the cabinets. In fact, Thorn was downright giddy to learn that the inn would be mostly empty…until he discovered Reena had offered to babysit the chiweenie so Kip could go to the competition. Then he mumbled something under his breath about Wayfarers turning into a zoo.

Janice could tell that Winnie was a nervous wreck, so she did her best to calm and encourage her as they made the drive. Along the way, they played worship songs and hymns. Once Winnie started singing, she seemed to calm down. Worship always seemed to have that effect on her.

Once they arrived at the event, Winnie and Sandie disappeared among the finalists and Janice, Tess, and LuAnn went in search of Georgia and Kip, who had made the journey in his truck.

Janice didn't have to travel very far before she stumbled into Kip. He had discovered the snack bar area and was loaded down with goodies—a bag of popcorn, a corndog, and a huge glass of lemonade.

She kept a watchful eye out for Hank Clive but didn't see him. In this crowd, who could find anyone they were looking for?

The emcee took the stage and got the ball rolling. Janice recognized him at once as the same short, overly happy man who had emceed the last event. He seemed to be right at home on the stage as he welcomed folks from all over the state to the Rising Star finals. Once the competition got underway, Janice was glued to the goings-on on stage. She snapped photos right and left as Winnie worked on her key lime pie and Sandie sat nearby, in case she was needed.

"How do you think she's doing?" Tess asked after they watched Winnie drop an empty mixing bowl.

"I'd say she's a jumble of nerves, if such a thing can be gathered from the way she's handling the equipment."

"Sandie is really watching her, ready in case she's needed for anything." This observation came from Georgia, who was holding hands with Kip.

"They're a good pair," LuAnn observed. "I'm sorry about your wrist, Georgia, but I'm kind of glad it worked out like this. I think God is really going to bring a strong friendship out of all of this."

Janice agreed. Still, she couldn't stop that nagging feeling that Hank Clive was somewhere nearby, possibly up to mischief. She craned her neck to see if he was anywhere near the stage but couldn't see over the very tall woman in front of her. Hopefully he wasn't backstage this time.

The pie category forged ahead, and before long all the entrants had their offerings on the judges' table. The three judges were apparently baking big shots, though Janice had never heard of any of them. The woman with the white hair looked familiar, but the younger man did not. And she'd certainly never seen that guy with the psychedelic shirt before. She would have remembered him.

"Oh, the judges really seem to like Winnie's key lime pie!" Georgia let out a little squeal followed by a rousing "Go, Winnie!"

Tess, who was standing in front of Georgia, jabbed her fingers in her ears. "Warn a person before you do that next time!"

Georgia giggled. "Yes, ma'am." She whispered, "Go Winnie!" and started nibbling on her popcorn again.

It didn't take long for the judges to decide. They gave the white ribbon to a man with an apple pie. The red ribbon went to a woman who'd made a peach pie. Then, with great fanfare, the emcee lifted the blue ribbon high.

"The Rising Star Company is proud to present this blue ribbon to the baker who gave us the most delectable key lime pie any of us have ever eaten. Congratulations to Winnie Washington of Wayfarers Inn in Marietta!"

The shouts and cheers rang out like fireworks popping on the Fourth of July. Now Janice had to stick her fingertips in her ears to drown out the celebration. Oh, but she kept her eyes wide open as Winnie took the ribbon in hand and lifted it high for all to see. Then Winnie turned and threw her arms around Sandie, who burst into tears.

"Well, if that isn't the sweetest sight I've ever seen." Janice dabbed at her eyes. "Will you go figure?"

"I knew they'd make a good team." Georgia snapped a picture with her phone. "I just knew it!"

Moments later Sandie cleared and prepped Winnie's station in preparation for the bread competition. Thinking of bread reminded Janice of Hank Clive. She still couldn't find him in the crowd. Near the stage on the right a man maneuvered a large television camera. Also near the front of the stage, a couple of professional photographers snapped photos. But none of them looked like Hank. Not even close.

Janice whispered a prayer for Winnie's safety. If that man had somehow made it backstage...no, she wouldn't think like that. Surely the contest officials were standing guard to make sure no monkey business took place.

Just as the bread competition got underway, Janice turned to face Kip and Georgia, her concerns amping up. "Have either of you seen Hank Clive since you got here?"

Kip shook his head. "Nope. I've had my eyes peeled since we got here."

"And I talked to the security guard before the contest started," Georgia added. "Even showed him a picture. Told him to be on the lookout."

"That was a smart idea, Georgia," LuAnn said. "I wish I'd thought of that."

"I checked out the press area when we arrived," Janice said. "Seemed like the most logical place. But he wasn't there, at least not at the time. I just hope he's not sabotaging Winnie's efforts by sending more of those messages."

"We know he's here somewhere," Tess said. "He made a point of telling us that."

Yes. He'd made a point of telling them he would be in Columbus.

Nagging concerns latched on to Janice and wouldn't let go. She tried to focus on Winnie, who was now slapping bread dough against the floured work space, but couldn't.

He said he would be here.

Perhaps that was just what he wanted them to believe.

Suddenly it all came into focus. Hank wanted them to think he would be here, but what if he never planned to come to Columbus at all? What if he had stayed behind for a reason? Had he, perchance, lured Reena to Wayfarers, not just for a story about bread, but so he could get the one thing he really wanted?

The ring.

He wanted the ring.

Janice flew into action at once. She reached inside her purse and pulled out her phone, then turned to find a less crowded space. Unfortunately, she was wedged in on every side.

"Everything okay?" Tess shouted above the roar of the crowd.

Janice shook her head and punched in the number to the inn.

Robin answered on the third ring.

"Oh, hey, Janice. How's it going? How's Winnie doing?"

"She won the pie category easily with her key lime. But that's not why I'm calling, Robin. I want you to listen to me closely, okay?"

"I can barely make out what you're saying. Is she doing the bread category now? I'm so glad she decided to go with the Parker House rolls. They're really yummy."

"Robin, please stop!" Janice shouted into the phone, "Listen closely. I'm calling the police. They should be there any moment!"

This certainly got Tess's and LuAnn's attention. They both turned to look at her. Janice held up an index finger, as if to say, "Give me a minute," then turned her attention to Robin so that she could give further instructions. "Do me a favor, and don't let Reena out of your sight."

"Oh, she's right here, petting the dog. We're waiting on that reporter to show up."

"What reporter?"

"You know…" Robin's voice faded as the crowd began to cheer for one of the contestants onstage. "That guy from the *Times*? He called and said he's coming over here around five o'clock to take photos of the inn. Said he wasn't able to make it to Columbus for the finals, so this is the next best thing."

"Robin, that man is not to be trusted. Do not—I repeat, do not—let him into the inn."

"You want me to bar the doors?" Robin laughed. "Really?"

"Really." Janice spoke with as much firmness as she could muster. "Don't let him in. And for pity's sake, don't let Reena know he's on his way. She'll be in a tizzy."

"She sure doesn't seem like she's in a tizzy. She's just sitting in the lobby, petting Kip's dog."

"Whatever you do, don't let Hank Clive in. Promise me."

"I promise. I'll ask Thorn to stand guard." Robin sounded as if she was half-joking, so Janice decided to take one further step.

"Do that, and call Brad Grimes, and ask him to come to the inn to be with you, And tell Reena to get all of her jewelry, including the gold wedding ring, out of her room."

"Gold wedding ring?"

"Hide all of it in the safe for us. Now. And please, make Reena stay in the office until this is over. After she puts the ring in the safe, I mean. I'll call the police and tell them about Hank coming. They will know what to do."

"O-okay."

Janice ended the call, and Tess looked at her, wide-eyed. "Why are we calling the police?" she shouted. Her elevated pitch got the attention of several people standing close by. They all looked Janice and Tess's way, and before long a hum went through the crowd: "Police? Someone called the police?"

"Goodness gracious goat!" Janice searched her phone for the number to the police station in Marietta then quickly made the call. Officer Randy Lewis was on the line with her a minute later, and she explained the situation.

"There's no law against going to a public café, Janice," Randy said. "If I catch him on the Wayfarers property, there's not much I can do."

"Can't you hold him, based on what I've just told you? He put those notes in the bread, I'm telling you."

"There are notes in the bread?" A woman standing to Janice's left looked her way, eyes widening. "What sort of notes?"

"Not the bread they're baking now," LuAnn tried to explain. "Other bread. In another town."

With the wave of a hand, Janice tried to get the ladies to hold the noise down so she could hear Randy. He agreed to go to the inn later that afternoon and keep an eye on things. She told him where to go when he got there.

Now if only this competition would come to an end so Janice and the others could head back to Wayfarers before anything awful happened. She would feel a thousand times better if she could just get back home again.

CHAPTER TWENTY-NINE

J anice might have surpassed the speed limit a little bit on the drive back to Marietta, but she just couldn't seem to help herself. Her foot kept a steady pressure on the accelerator.

"Whoa, Nellie!" Winnie put her hands up in the air as they changed lanes. "Is this a NASCAR race?"

"No." Janice tapped the brakes and slowed down. "Sorry. Didn't mean to alarm you."

"It's going to be okay, Janice," Tess said. "Robin would've called us if Hank Clive showed up. You know that."

"I still don't understand why he's headed to the inn at all." Winnie held her trophy close and smiled. "If he wanted pictures of me taking the big prize, he should've come to Columbus."

Janice didn't bother explaining that Hank Clive really wasn't interested in Winnie or her prize. No point in bringing her down from that cloud she happened to be floating on at the moment.

"We're so proud of you, Winnie," she said and then turned long enough to offer her friend an encouraging smile.

"Thanks. I'm giddy." Winnie laughed, then turned toward the back seat. "Sandie, you can be my baking assistant any time you like."

"Thanks. I had the time of my life. That was a blast, Winnie."

Janice tried to keep the conversation focused on Winnie as she made the trip back to Wayfarers but had to switch gears when she pulled into the parking lot and saw three police cars filling the spots closest to the door.

"Oh my." Tess's words from the back seat pretty much spoke what everyone was feeling.

Janice parked and bounded from the car. When she made it to the door, two officers shoved through with Hank Clive in handcuffs. He took one look at the Inn Crowd and glared.

Randy led Hank toward a patrol car and opened the back door. "We caught him upstairs in Mrs. Newberry's room. Your instincts were right, Janice. But thanks to your call, I was there in Mrs. Newberry's room. I watched as he broke in and started riffling through her things. He got into the inn through the kitchen."

"Of course he did," Janice said. "Just like the night he broke in with twelve loaves of bread." She turned to Winnie. "You didn't forget to lock the kitchen door that night, Winnie. Hank came to switch your loaves with the loaves he'd put messages in."

From the back seat of the patrol car, Hank Clive started grumbling. "I have the right to an attorney," he called out. "I know my rights."

"You'll get to make that call when we arrive at the station, Mr. Clive," Randy said. "Until then, I would suggest you say very little."

"I'll be happy to tell you what happened," Janice said. "He can tell his side of things when he's got an attorney present." She turned to face Hank, who continued to scowl at her. "You wanted to hurt our business, to scare people away. That's why you put the messages in the bread."

"Why would I want to do that?"

"I don't know for sure. Maybe for a better story for your paper? And you wanted to keep a closer watch on Reena, in the hopes she would lead you to that ring and possibly her other jewels, besides."

"Ring? What ring?" He feigned innocence, but Janice could see right through him.

"You know very well what ring—the one your great-great-great grandfather Theodore Clive sent to Birdie Atkinson in 1860. A gold wedding band that traveled from your hometown of Lexington, Kentucky, all the way to Pittsburgh. The ring you insisted she bring to Wayfarers with her when you sent the invitation on that gray stationery."

"Your storytelling skills are stellar, Janice." Hank rolled his eyes. "Maybe you should work for the paper."

"No, thanks. I have enough drama in my life already. But I think I've hit this nail right on the head. You planned today down to a T—it was a day we were all out of town. I'd say a lot of thought and planning went into this."

He grunted. "Those Newberrys stole more than just his ring. They took the only thing my great-great-great-grandfather ever loved."

"Birdie?" Janice asked.

"Yes, Birdie. And taking her away from him changed everything."

"How so?" Tess asked.

"You rip a man's heart out of him and then ask a question like that? Teddy married, had children, but was never happy. Never. Did you know he took his own life at the age of thirty-three? Bet you don't read about that in that stupid diary of yours, because it's not in there. So, go on, paint Prudence as a hero because she baked a loaf of bread and sent the ring. But little good it did Teddy Clive in the end."

Janice was stunned. Theodore killed himself?

"He was never happy," Hank grumbled. "My great-great-grandfather was raised without his dad, and that affected him greatly. By the time my father was born, the Clive men were bitter and hard. And all because of the Newberry family. That ring belongs in our family. It was Teddy Clive's, and now it's rightfully mine, since I'm the only living heir."

"You can tell your story from a cell," Randy said. "We've got him on breaking and entering and attempted robbery. There will be more charges after we figure out how to get a confession out of him about those messages in the bread." He scratched his head. "Never arrested anyone for that one before. Not even sure where to start."

"Thank you, Randy," Janice said. "I need to get inside to Reena. I'm sure she's beside herself with worry over all of this."

"No, I'm not!" Reena came from the inn, carrying Dobbins in her arms. "I watched the whole thing. It was better than a soap opera."

"Better than a soap opera, indeed," Janice said…and then laughed.

CHAPTER THIRTY

August 30, 1860

As the early evening hours crept over the town of Marietta, Prudence took leave of the Riverfront House. She found herself at the river's edge and paused to take in the colors of the setting sun over the spot where the two rivers merged together. Only a heavenly Creator could make colors like that—a magnificent convergence of red, gold, orange, and yellow, all mixed in with blue.

Prudence's thoughts traveled to Birdie and Theodore. They had become storybook characters to her, people she would likely never meet. But at the moment, they were as real as if they were standing right here next to her. Were their lives meant to merge forever, as the Ohio melded into the Muskingum? Or would the pain of separation wedge them apart forever? Would the love between them be strong enough to cross the divide between North and South?

Prudence walked along the river's edge, one quiet step after another. She thought about her deep love for Jason.

How her heart ached for that man whenever they were apart. To be separated from one you love must be awful. How must Birdie feel, so far away from the one she loved? Would her story end, as all good stories did, with a joyous reunion?

War was coming—and soon. Everyone spoke of it in hushed whispers. Like a mighty river, it could not be stopped. Before long, it would wash over them all. In the quiet hours of the night, Jason whispered his thoughts about the nation's great divide, convinced it would only deepen with time. She fought it with every fiber of her being. No nation should be ripped in two. No heart should be divided.

And there, in the midst of it all, this overwhelming call of God on her life to play a role, to busy herself for His kingdom, His people. To stand in the gap.

There would always be Theodores. There would always be Birdies. These precious souls would look to her, to Jason, to others of similar mindset, to right the wrongs of a nation bent on division. They would cry out for help and pray that someone was listening.

She paused and lifted her hands to the sky, as if in surrender. The words "Yes, Lord!" came out as a whispered prayer, an affirmation that she would—she could—do whatever He asked her to do. Every knock on the door, every hushed conversation, would serve as a reminder that her life was not her own.

"It was never meant to be my own." She said the words aloud to the evening breeze. It lifted and carried them far away from where she now stood, perhaps all the way to

Pennsylvania, to a young woman not so very unlike herself, one who loved a man with her whole heart.

"What has Thee called me to do, Lord?" Prudence whispered. "Open my eyes to see, I pray."

The answer landed on her heart like a feather lighting on the ground below.

Love.

Love bound all things together. It offered hope to all who would listen. It gave courage where courage was due. And love was meant to be spread like a seed—as far as the hand could fling it.

CHAPTER THIRTY-ONE

The days following Winnie's big win at state finals turned out to be filled with chaos and confusion, albeit most of it delightful in nature. Saturday night Margaret called to say that Justin had inspected the cookstove again, and the fire wasn't sabotage. The official conclusion was "These things happen when you work with old stuff." By Monday morning the café was once again filled with guests who couldn't wait to taste her scrumptious offerings. And once the *Times* ran their story on Hank Clive, most of those who had canceled their reservations rebooked. Janice could hardly believe how seamlessly everything was coming together. She also couldn't believe how tired they all were as they worked together toward their goals.

Things slowed down a couple of days before Reena was scheduled to go back to Pennsylvania. She was taking with her a copy of Prudence's diary as a memento, as well as the ring, which she now wore around her neck on a chain. Janice decided to throw a going-away party for the now well-loved Reena on Monday night. She invited several of Reena's new friends, including Sandie and Kip. She also asked Brad to join them. They all met in the café at six o'clock.

Janice waited until everyone was served and then stood and clinked her water glass with her knife. "Attention, everyone!" she said. "I want to say a few words."

She shared from the heart about how much Reena meant to her and then passed the metaphorical microphone to Tess, then LuAnn, then Winnie, then Sandie, then on around the table to Georgia and Kip. By the time everyone finished, Reena was awash in tears.

"I'm just so grateful you all welcomed me like this," she said. "It feels so wonderful to have your love reciprocated." Her eyes flooded once again. "I guess that's how Birdie felt, even though she and Theodore were separated. She knew in her heart that she had once been loved by the one she loved in return."

"This is kind of a twisted love story," Brad said as he jabbed his fork into his roasted chicken.

"Right?" Kip agreed. "Who needs made-for-TV movies when you've got real chick flicks like this?"

"A love story is a love story, whether it's written in 1860 or the twenty-first century, Kip," Janice responded. "And you're right, gentlemen, it's a twisted tale, but it's also a good reminder that there are many different types of love—the love between friends, like we have with all of you, the love of a man and a woman—like Theodore had with Birdie—and ultimately, the love of God, who was—like William—willing to lay down His life for His friends…us."

"Whoa." Kip gave her an admiring look. "You almost turned that into a sermon, Mrs. Eastman."

Janice laughed. "Sorry. I didn't mean to. Guess all those years of being a pastor's wife paid off." She paused and thought about those years. "You might be surprised how many sermons I helped with, how many folks I counseled. A pastor's wife is in ministry too, I promise you. And, speaking of sermons, I think it's time for a heart-to-heart about something else as well."

"About what?" Tess asked.

"R & R."

"A heart-to-heart about R & R?" Tess smiled. "Is that a new radio jingle or something?"

"No, it's a new way of life, one I hope we will adopt before we all drop to the ground from exhaustion."

"Amen," Brad said. "Would you throw in a nap for me too?"

LuAnn chuckled.

Tess's eyes widened. "But, Janice, we just booked up through Thanksgiving. This is no time to rest on our laurels. We've got work to do."

"Laurels?" Kip looked up from his food. "What's laurels?"

"From what I can gather, it's something you sit on," Brad said, and kept on eating.

"I'm not suggesting we rest on our laurels," Janice explained. "It's just that we remember to take time out to thoroughly and completely rest—not just our bodies, but our minds and our souls. If we say we're taking a rest day, let's take a rest day. And if we say we're off the clock at a certain time, we should be off the clock. And for the record, I say we cut back on the marketing. It's working a little too well."

"Is that even possible?" Robin asked.

Janice couldn't help but smile as she said, "Like LuAnn said, we don't want our rabbits to multiply too quickly."

"Rabbits." Kip snorted, and Georgia jabbed him with her elbow.

"There may come a time when we need to think up new marketing strategies," Janice said. "Some real zingers, even. But I suppose we can just play it by ear till then."

"What was the tagline from that one movie?" Tess asked. "Something like, 'If we build it, they will come'? Let's just let that be our motto from now on, shall we?"

LuAnn nodded. "In other words, we need to trust God more and stop taking things into our own hands so much."

"Yes, I guess that's what I mean." Janice said.

Tess reached for her water glass. "I suppose it is a little arrogant and prideful to say we should try to handle things on our own when the God of the universe is right there, hoping we'll call on Him."

Janice offered her friends an encouraging smile. "Exactly. Let's leave the ball in His court, so to speak. We'll get things done. But I, for one, am ready to just be a Mary, not a Martha."

"I thought her first name was Janice?" Kip said to Brad, then shrugged and reached for his fork.

Tess leaned forward. "Winnie, you'll be able to get some R & R soon, won't you? I remember something about a cruise as part of the prize package, don't I?"

Winnie turned to her. "You remember right, Tess. Unfortunately, it's not until early next year. That's when the celebrity chefs they booked could get away for it." She sighed. "I'm a bit disappointed. I was ready to learn some new techniques from some masters."

"Speaking of learning from the masters..." Georgia pushed herself to a standing position, as if ready to make an announcement of some sort. She straightened her shoulders and cleared her throat. "I would like to say something."

Everyone stopped talking and focused on her.

"When I first came here, I thought my lessons would be all about scones and pies and cinnamon rolls. I thought I would go back to Akron with new recipes and techniques." She looked around the table. "And I will. You all know I think Winnie is the best. But I had no idea I'd learn from all of you about how to treat people, how to pray for people, how to have faith that things will work out." She wiped her eyes and drew a shaky breath.

In the middle of the hugs that followed, Winnie stopped cold and pointed at Georgia's arm. "Wait a minute. Why aren't you wearing your sling?"

"My what?" Georgia glanced down at her wrist and then let out a yelp. "Oh, oops! I forgot to put it on after my shower this afternoon."

"I saw you using that arm just now," Winnie said. "Saw it with my own eyes. Show me how you move that wrist, girl."

With a loud groan, Georgia extended her arm and wiggled it back and forth.

"What's this I'm looking at?" Winnie asked. "Either God has miraculously healed you, or you've tried to pull one over on me."

"Maybe I exaggerated a little," Georgia said. "It probably wasn't sprained badly enough to keep me from helping you at the competition. But I really did trip over the dog, didn't I, Kip?" She gave him a pouty look. "And it did hurt...a little."

"So, you thought it'd be fun to get Sandie to take your place?" Winnie asked.

Sandie started laughing and couldn't seem to stop. When she finally came up for air she thanked Georgia for her generous gesture. "I'm not sure anyone's ever gone to such trouble to make sure I was included before. I'm really grateful, Georgia. Working with Winnie was a dream come true."

"Really? Working with little old me?" Winnie pointed to herself.

Sandie nodded. "You bet. Now, if you'd show me that technique you used with your pie crust, I'd be honored. We didn't learn that in culinary school."

"Well, of course you didn't learn that in that hoity-toity culinary school, girl," Winnie countered. "That's the sort of thing passed down from grandmother to mother to child."

She stopped at once, realizing what she'd said. "Oh, I'm sorry, honey. I plumb forgot about your mama."

Sandie's eye misted over, but just as quickly she seemed to push her sadness away. "Guess you'll just have to teach me those things, Winnie. If you're willing, I mean."

"If I'm willing? Well, I'm always happy to pass down baking secrets, as long as you don't advertise them."

"Ugh." Tess slapped herself on the forehead. "Advertise. Don't use that word!"

"I would like to go on record as saying I don't know how or when I'll ever use up that lifetime supply of flour and baking powder from Rising Star." Winnie shook her head. "I'll need a storage facility to house it all."

"I've got a huge storage closet at my bakery," Sandie said.

"I'll make you a deal...you store it, you keep half of it. You did earn it, you know."

"Really?" Sandie's mouth fell open. "You mean that?"

"Sure. Between us, maybe we'll make a dent in it."

The two women took to talking about baking and before long were in a world of their own. Janice looked over just in time to see Reena passing a nibble of chicken to the chiweenie, who had been resting underneath the table. The little pup jumped up and down until he finally caught the treat in his mouth.

"Come to Mama, Beauvine." Reena patted her knees, and the pup jumped up into her lap. He turned around a couple of times and finally settled down.

"Bovine?" Brad asked. "Like a cow?"

"Beau. B-e-a-u." Reena scratched the pup behind the ears, and within seconds the little love had nearly fallen asleep.

Tess clucked her tongue. "Why, Reena Newberry, I do believe you've gone and fallen for that pooch."

Reena released a slow breath and then shifted her gaze down to the dog, who had taken to snoring. "I've never had a pet before."

"Not ever?" Janice asked.

"No. Not ever. Back in my day, you didn't have animals in the house. Well, not unless you were the queen of England or something, and even she has people to take care of them for her, if you know what I mean."

Janice smiled at her. "True."

"Because I wasn't raised with them, I've really never been around them much. Beauvine here is the first canine who's ever won me over."

"What about Huck?" LuAnn asked.

Reena's nose wrinkled. "He's fine, as dogs go, but this little guy has won my heart."

Georgia quirked a brow, and a hint of a smile tipped up the edges of her lips. "You're talking as if you plan to keep him, Miss Reena."

Mist covered the edges of Reena's lashes. "As much as that would please me, I could never take him from Kip."

"Actually, I'm not able to keep him much longer," Kip explained with a shrug. "Remember, I said when he showed up that I couldn't take him for long."

"Are you saying Beauvine is in need of a new owner?" Reena's eyes sparkled. "Really, truly?"

Kip gestured to the contented pooch. "I'd say he's already found one."

Janice couldn't help but smile. "I'm not sure that dog will ever have a better home than the one you can offer him, Reena."

Her eyes lit with merriment. "Oh, he'll have full run of the house. I'm sure it'll drive my housekeeper bonkers, but I don't care about that." Reena took to petting the dog again, then suddenly sat up straight in her chair. "Oh my goodness, I have the best idea! Winnie, these gals are hoping you'll take some time off to rest, and I've got just the place. My home in Pennsylvania is divine. It's a lovely, spacious country home. Oh, you should see it this time of year. The gardens are amazing. The flowers are still in bloom. I just know you'll love it."

"What will I do there?" Winnie asked. "Cook for you?"

Reena looked shocked by this notion. "For goodness' sake, no. I've got a wonderful woman named Nelly who does my cooking. You're going to love her."

"Then what will I do with my time?"

"Exactly what I've been doing here," Reena said. "You'll rest. You'll sleep till noon and have your meals brought to you at whatever time you please. You'll start a diary. You'll be my guest."

"Sleep till noon?" Winnie's eyes widened. "I can't even imagine that."

"Once you try it, you'll never go back." Reena chuckled. "But, seriously...I could use the company. And you'll just love Pennsylvania. Come and stay for as long as you like."

Winnie's gaze traveled from Janice to Tess to LuAnn, then back to Reena. "I'm not sure these ladies could do without me for very long."

"There's still over a full week left in August," Tess said. "Take a whole week. We'll manage, I promise."

"But so many people have made reservations to stay at the inn."

"Most of them start in September. Don't fret, Winnie. Just go and relax."

"I'm not sure I know how."

"All the more reason to give it a go." Reena wagged her finger in Winnie's face. "And I promise not to bother you. Beauvine and I will be so quiet you won't even know we're in the house."

The pup gave a little yip, as if to defy her.

"Are you serious, Reena? If so, then I accept!" Winnie rose and gave the woman a hug that lasted a good long while.

Reena took the conversation off in a completely different direction, talking about all of the amazing places she wanted to take Winnie while visiting. Then she laid out a detailed plan about Beauvine's new accommodations, right down to his bed and outfits. "I never saw myself as a dog lover before, but I suppose everyone my age needs a pet. It's quite therapeutic to have a little doggie to love on."

Janice couldn't help but agree. In that moment, as she watched Reena snuggle her new pet, she was overcome with emotion. The words she had spoken to the others now held her thoughts captive. There really were so many different types of love in this world. The blossoming love between a young woman and young man. The steadfast bond between a husband and wife. Joyous friendships, which spanned the years. Everlasting love between God and people. Even the adoration of a precious older woman for her newly adopted pup.

As Janice took it all in, she considered how Prudence had been right all along. Surely God's love calls people together, unites their differences, and joins their hearts.

Dear Reader,

I'm in love with all things baking! My kitchen is a holy, "set apart" place, where I can rest my heart and mind and spend time with the Lord. There, with the tantalizing aromas of snickerdoodles filling the air, I can forget about my troubles, escape my deadlines, and just be. It's also a place where I can spend time with my grandchildren, passing on family recipes and sharing my passion for cakes, cookies, and other tasty delights.

Adding a baking-themed story to the Wayfarers Inn collection was pure joy! How fun to plop Winnie in the middle of a big baking competition where she could shine like a star. Perhaps I was living vicariously through her. The only competitions I've entered have been at my church, but I did come home with a few ribbons. There's nothing like a pat on the back to make a gal think she's got talent!

What drew me to this story idea was the notion that Winnie has such an amazing kitchen at her disposal. I could picture her there, hovering over Big Red, baking up delicious pies, amazing cakes, and yummy cookies. I could imagine Janice, LuAnn, and Tess cheering her on as she prepped for the big competition. I could see the guests, wide-eyed with wonder, making their choices from her vast display of goodies. Most of all, I could see Winnie getting the pats on the back and the recognition she deserves for a job well done. And I could see all of this wrapped up in a story filled with plenty of twists and turns.

I hope you found great joy in reading *The Secret Ingredient*. I certainly enjoyed writing it! Now that you've reached the end, why don't you settle back, grab a cookie and a cup of tea, and savor the moment!

Thank you so much for reading.

Janice Thompson

About the Author

Award-winning author Janice Thompson got her start in the industry writing plays and musical comedies for the stage. Janice has published over 110 books for the Christian market, crossing genre lines to write cozy mysteries, historicals, romances, nonfiction books, devotionals, children's books, and more. Janice is passionate about her faith and does all she can to share the joy of the Lord with others, which is why she particularly enjoys writing. She lives in Spring, Texas, where she leads a rich life with her family, a host of writing friends, and three mischievous dogs. When she's not busy writing or playing with her nine grandchildren, Janice can be found in the kitchen, baking specialty cakes and cookies for friends and loved ones. No matter what she's cooking up—books, cakes, cookies, or mischief—she does her best to keep the Lord at the center of it all.

A Culinary Trip Down
the Railroad

Have you ever given thought to what the slaves ate as they traveled northward on the Underground Railroad? Food was often scarce as they made their way toward freedom. Many runaways hunted for small game as they passed through dense forests. Squirrels, rabbits—anything would do. Others survived on berries or herbs, which could be foraged as they traveled. Still others caught and ate fish from the streams and rivers they traversed.

Perhaps the most famous food story came from none other than Harriet Tubman, herself. With thirteen trips "down to Egypt" she had plenty of opportunity to consider food sources for her rescued slaves. More often than not, she would forage for things like black cherry, paw-paw, and sassafras. Once, while purchasing two chickens at a market, she very nearly came face-to-face with a former overseer. She needed to distract him in a hurry, so she released one of the squawking chickens and made quite a show out of giving chase to the bird. This caused a chaotic scene, giving Harriet the perfect opportunity to slip away unseen. Talk about ingenious!

Harriet wasn't the only one who made sure the runaways were cared for. As travelers made their various stops along the railroad, they were provided with foods for the journey. Some of the most common included roasted potatoes, both white and sweet. These could be carried and eaten without utensils. They were also given muffins, particularly cornbread, a staple. Anything that could be held in the hand and eaten in a hurry would work, so foods like beef jerky were especially good. And, as the season allowed, many carried fruit as well.

No matter what they ate as they traveled, "passengers" along the Underground Railroad found a way to use their wits to fill their stomachs.

Something Delicious from our Wayfarers Inn Friends

Winnie's Snickerdoodles

Cookies

1 cup shortening	2 teaspoon cream of tartar
2 eggs	1 teaspoon baking soda
1 cup sugar	½ teaspoon salt
2¾ cups flour	

1. Cream together shortening, eggs, and sugar.
2. In separate bowl sift together flour, cream of tartar, baking soda, and salt.
3. Combine wet and dry mixtures. Shape dough into 1-inch balls. Roll in cinnamon and sugar mixture (2 T sugar/2 T cinnamon).
4. Place 2 inches apart on ungreased cookie sheet. Bake at 350 degrees for 10 to 11 minutes.

Read on for a sneak peek of another exciting book
in the Secrets of Wayfarers Inn series!

SUBMERGED SURPRISES
by Ocieanna Fleiss

So you can see." LuAnn peered at the small audience crowded into Marietta Historical Society's wood-paneled meeting room. "Wayfarers Inn's rich Underground Railroad history serves to fascinate, illuminate, and inspire even the most modern minds." This was the last in her three-part lecture series on the history of Marietta. She'd walked through early settlements, the War for Independence with the famous visits of George Washington and Lafayette, Marietta's expansion after the war, and its abolitionist roots. She ended with the Underground Railroad history. She thought her inn's unique history would be fitting. She'd told her friends and co-owners, Tess Wallace and Janice Eastman, she was saving the best for last. They'd readily agreed.

Even now, Tess's smiling face in the audience displayed her ever-present support as she filmed the lecture on her phone. Janice was back at the inn. It was her turn to keep things running. She'd watch the video later.

"Any questions?" LuAnn scanned the room, her gaze landing on the other member of her support system, Brad Grimes. Their friendship had grown over the last year. She depended on him almost as much as Tess and Janice. How grateful she was for his presence in her life. In the instant she glanced at him, he turned to his phone, which apparently had vibrated. A frown spread over his face for a moment before his reassuring smile returned.

Looking around, she recognized most of the faces as locals, but one young woman sitting next to their friend Margaret Ashworth, the historical society's director, looked unfamiliar. Throughout the lecture, she'd been very attentive, especially for a young person, even taking notes. Most of the historical society folk were of an older generation.

After taking a couple of questions, LuAnn paused, waiting for others. A hand went up toward the back belonging to a woman with straight brown hair who had been looking at her notes most of the lecture. She now lifted her chin, and a gleam shone from her eyes that sent a happy thrill of recognition to LuAnn's heart. "Ashley?"

The woman nodded and then smiled with a hint of mischievousness. "Miss Sherrill. I was wondering, you mentioned the Underground Railroad history of Wayfarers Inn. Are you available to discuss this in more depth?"

LuAnn tilted her head toward her former student, chuckling inwardly at her mock formality. "Yes, I'm happy to share the inn's rich history. Feel free to contact me, and I'll be happy to set something up."

"Thank you very much. I certainly will do that." Ashley smiled.

"I look forward to it." LuAnn picked up her pencil and notebook. "If there are no more questions, I'll close with this quote from the famous Underground Railroad conductor, Harriet Tubman. 'Every great dream begins with a dreamer. Always remember, you have within you the strength, the patience, and the passion to reach for the stars to change the world.' Thank you."

The crowd clapped as LuAnn moved to the side table where Margaret had displayed an offering of books about Marietta's history as well as some travel guides—none of them hers. LuAnn sighed. She'd always wanted to write a book. It would be amazing to have her own book sitting amongst the others on the table. Hers would be a novel, of course. Her love for Marietta comingled for a moment with the book dream, birthing a new thought. A novel with the setting in Marietta? Her heart raced at the idea. But writing a novel was a long-ago fantasy. She brushed the thought aside.

Tess approached, but LuAnn's gaze snagged on Brad, who lingered by the door trying to catch her attention. He tilted his head apologetically and pointed toward the door. He had to go. Disappointment touched her heart, but he mimicked a phone, reassuring her that he'd call. She knew he would.

Tess waited, apparently noticing LuAnn's attention toward Brad. "Aw, he has to go?"

"Yeah. He'll call me later though," LuAnn answered with a grin.

"You could tell that from a look?" Tess asked.

"And a few hand motions." She leaned into Tess's hug. "I'm glad you made it."

"You did great. You're a natural at this stuff."

"Thanks. Once a teacher, always a teacher, I guess."

"That's right."

At that moment, Ashley orbited LuAnn and Tess, and LuAnn stepped forward. "Ashley?" She pulled her into a hug. "I can't believe you're here. Sneaky of you raising your hand at the last minute like that."

Ashley grinned. "I thought it would be fun to surprise you."

From LuAnn's memory of Ashley sitting in her history and English classes, she guessed Ashley to be in her late thirties or early forties. They had kept in touch now and then via email and social media, but she hadn't seen her in person for years. "You look amazing."

"Hi, I'm—" Tess started.

"Oh my! I forgot to introduce you." LuAnn pointed toward Tess. "This is my friend and business partner, Tess."

Tess shook Ashley's hand. "It's nice to meet you."

"What brings you to Marietta?" LuAnn continued. "I would have thought this would be the busy time of year for a Princeton history professor."

Ashley nodded. "It normally is, but I'm on a sabbatical right now."

"That's awesome," Tess commented. "How long do they give you?"

"Would you believe a whole year?" she said. "I'm planning to finish my third book—among other things."

"Wow. Three books. Good for you." LuAnn smiled. "You always were my star student."

"You inspired me." Ashley tilted her head. "You really did."

Words LuAnn's teacher heart loved to hear. "Thank you for saying so." She eyed her prestigious friend. "So, what's the other thing you're throwing yourself into?"

Ashley's lips curved in an excited smile. "Apparently there's a historic site here called the Castle."

"We know about that place. It was built in the 1850s. Isn't that right?"

"That's the one. They're doing some rehabilitation of the brickwork and the outside grounds. While they're doing that"— she rubbed her palms together—"the inside is all mine."

"What do you mean?" LuAnn asked.

"The museum board hired me to go through the rooms and rewrite the historic plaques. I get to fact check, rework the wording, and also dig up any more historic nuggets about the place. They're also having me do full profiles on the owners and even write a script for a short documentary they're going to show visitors."

All the history talk made LuAnn's pulse race. "Sounds like a lot of fun."

"A lot of work," Tess put in.

"Both," Ashley agreed. "But I'm up for it. It'll be a nice change from the classroom."

"I can understand that," LuAnn said.

"Where are you staying?" Tess asked.

LuAnn peered at her friend. "I would have noticed your name in the reservation book. Don't tell me you came to Marietta and are not staying at our inn."

Ashley cringed. "I'm afraid I procrastinated, and when I checked, you were booked up. I figured it would give me a chance to surprise you, but I admit, I was a little disappointed. I've heard such amazing things about it."

LuAnn eyed Tess. "Do we have any openings?"

"I do think we're pretty booked up, but..." Tess's eyes twinkled. "The Johnsons in Apples and Cinnamon are checking out tomorrow instead of Thursday. So..."

"So you have an opening?" Ashley asked.

"Sounds like tomorrow we will," LuAnn answered. "Come by at noon or so. We'll get you checked in, and you and I can have lunch. Sound good?"

"Absolutely. I better head out into your gorgeous late-summer afternoon now. I want to stop by the Castle before it gets too late."

After Ashley departed, Margaret stepped into the gap left by her. The young woman LuAnn had noticed stood next to her.

"Well," Margaret started, her head trembling slightly. "I don't want to interrupt, but I wanted to introduce you to my niece. She's my great-niece actually." Her wrinkled hand pointed toward the younger woman. "Dahlia. This is LuAnn Sherrill and Tess Wallace."

Margaret's niece tucked her wavy brown hair behind her ears as she stepped forward. "Hi." She smiled warmly. "I'm so glad to meet you. My aunt has told me all about you."

LuAnn eyed Tess questioningly. She didn't realize Margaret knew "all about" them.

Dahlia seemed to perceive LuAnn's doubt, and she giggled nervously. "I'm sorry. I don't mean everything. I'm just a big history nut, and she said you both own the inn. I'm so fascinated by its history." She pushed her dark-rimmed glasses up. "I admit. I'm an aspiring writer. I'd love to write a novel about your inn." She glanced at her hands. "I don't know. It's a dream, I guess. But history seems to be alive in this town."

LuAnn smiled more stiffly than she meant to. "That's... a great idea."

"You should come by some time," Tess offered. "We can give you a tour."

"Thanks."

Thinking the conversation was winding down, LuAnn edged away, but Margaret stopped her. "I have something else to tell you." Her eyes gleamed as she focused on LuAnn, then she shifted a glance toward Tess. "You might even like this."

LuAnn grinned at Tess, acknowledging the slight. "What is it?"

"Well." She began a slow march toward the stairs, accompanied by Dahlia.

LuAnn and Tess followed obediently.

They reached the musty downstairs room stacked with 1940s-looking metal shelves, perfectly ordered. Labeled plastic containers sat on the shelves, one of which sat on a small round table. Margaret grabbed her afghan from her desk in the corner and wrapped it around her shoulders. "It's always so chilly in this room, no matter how warm it is outside." She then returned to the table, pulled out a chair, and sat. Her gaze urged the others to join her.

As LuAnn sat down, she noticed the label on the plastic container. It said, "Marietta Times 1863 Sept-Oct." Old clippings about Marietta? What had Margaret found?

Margaret removed a worn manila folder labeled "Sept. 25." Cautiously, she lifted a clipping from the file and held it up.

"Gold Coins Lost in Marietta," the headline read.

LuAnn inspected the browned paper with its black courier script. "Gold coins?" She tilted her head toward Margaret. "Someone lost gold coins here?"

Margaret nodded, so LuAnn started to read.

Sources have confirmed that while the citizenry slept in Marietta, a Confederate delivery of gold coins was routed. At printing, the coins have not yet been found . . .

"I may not be a history buff," Tess said, "but this is pretty cool."

"It is." LuAnn's pulse sped. "It makes me want to go on a treasure hunt." She grabbed her phone from her pocket, thinking she'd take a photo, maybe post it on the Marietta history-lover's webpage she'd recently discovered.

After LuAnn took the picture, Margaret put the clipping back into its home in the folder while LuAnn watched mournfully. "I thought you would like it."

LuAnn slipped her phone back in her pocket. "Can I come back and study it more carefully?" she asked. "I'm so interested now."

"Of course. It's getting late, though."

"Four o'clock is not late, Aunt Maggie." Dahlia smiled at Margaret, who didn't seem to hear her.

LuAnn and Tess followed Margaret and Dahlia as they wandered upstairs. A wave of exhaustion hit LuAnn. She enjoyed speaking engagements like this, but they did wear her introverted self out. She took in a breath for strength, then turned to Tess.

"Let's get you home." Tess patted her shoulder. "I have a feeling Janice will have an early dinner waiting—or at least something delicious to fill our stomachs."

The thought of a delicacy made by their third business partner and friend brought a smile to LuAnn. "Nothing would be better." She grabbed her jacket, books, and lecture notes from the table where she'd left them and followed Tess out the door.

As they walked home, LuAnn posted a short note to her Marietta history-lovers group about the article Margaret had shown them. Her friends on there would love it—and possibly have information about it. If not the coins, at least more about the time period. Who knew?

An hour later, the Inn Crowd sat in their fourth-floor kitchen, sipping the last bits of their after-dinner iced tea.

"That was the perfect meal, Janice," LuAnn said. "That green goddess salad. And the beef panini. It was just delicious."

Janice folded her napkin and laid it on her plate, her eyes sparkling. "I thought it would be fitting. It's still warm, but I can feel fall in the air."

Tess nodded. "Me too. That and with school starting—Lizzie has the triplets in preschool. Can you believe it?"

Janice stood and collected the plates. "And my Larry's in first grade! Time flies by."

"All those years we were in the throes of teaching this time of year. Right Janice?" LuAnn interjected. "Seems like forever ago."

"Yeah." Janice peered out the window and sighed. "Do you miss it?"

LuAnn wrinkled her brow. "Not really."

Janice turned back to her, laughing. "Me neither. It was so much work."

"You two." Tess shook her head.

"Do you miss teaching at the community college?"

Tess pinched her lips together. "Not really. Running the inn is much more fun."

"It truly is," LuAnn agreed.

The three finished the dishes and headed to their sitting area. "Oh, by the way, how's the planning for the Taste of Marietta?" LuAnn asked. "That's this Saturday, right? I've been so preoccupied with these lectures—I'm afraid I haven't been much help."

Janice nodded. "Yeah. Winnie ordered the ingredients from Marcus today. I'm glad we're doing it. I always enjoy those events where you pay five dollars and get a sample of the different restaurants. I've tried things I never thought I would at those events." She chuckled.

"I remember," LuAnn put in. "You actually tried alligator that time." She joined in the laughter.

"And you said it tasted like chicken," Tess added.

Janice's eyes widened. "It really did!"

"Anyway." Tess returned the conversation to the topic at hand. "We should talk about who's going to take care of the inn while that's going on."

"Sounds good."

After finishing her evening chores, LuAnn settled into her apartment. She fell asleep wondering why Brad hadn't called.

The next morning, LuAnn glanced at her phone. Still no call from Brad. Why hadn't he called? He was usually so reliable. What could be going on?

After dressing, she joined Tess and Janice in the common room, and they went down the staircase to help Winnie with the guest breakfast. The inn was pretty full, so she knew it was all hands on deck this mornng.

About midway through the cafe service, LuAnn's phone rang. She glanced at it. Not Brad. It was a number she didn't recognize. She stepped behind the large antique desk, which had been a bar when the bottom floor of the inn was a saloon, and answered.

"Hi, Miss Sherrill," a young woman's voice started. It sounded worried, almost frantic. "I'm sorry to bother you—"

"Who is this?" LuAnn asked, glancing at Tess, who had just stepped out of the office.

"It's Dahlia. Oh, Miss Sherrill. I thought you would want to know…"

"Dahlia. Call me LuAnn."

Tess stepped closer. She must have noticed LuAnn's worried expression. Janice joined them.

"My aunt is gone."

"Margaret's gone?" LuAnn responded. "What do you mean?"

"I think…I think she was kidnapped."

A Note from the Editors

We hope you enjoy Secrets of Wayfarers Inn, created by the Books and Inspirational Media Division of Guideposts, a nonprofit organization that touches millions of lives every day through products and services that inspire, encourage, help you grow in your faith, and celebrate God's love in every aspect of your daily life.

Thank you for making a difference with your purchase of this book, which helps fund our many outreach programs to military personnel, prisons, hospitals, nursing homes, and educational institutions. To learn more, visit Guideposts Foundation.org.

We also maintain many useful and uplifting online resources. Visit Guideposts.org to read true stories of hope and inspiration, access OurPrayer network, sign up for free news-letters, download free e-books, join our Facebook community, and follow our stimulating blogs.

To learn about other Guideposts publications, including the best-selling devotional *Daily Guideposts*, go to ShopGuideposts .org, call (800) 932-2145, or write to Guideposts, PO Box 5815, Harlan, Iowa 51593.

Sign up for the
Guideposts Fiction Newsletter
and stay up to date on the books you love!

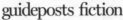

guideposts fiction
Inspiring reads chosen just for you!

What's New

Mysteries of Lancaster County

Welcome to Bird-in-Hand, Pennsylvania, a quaint village in the heart of Lancaster County's Amish Country. It's here, amid rolling green hills and well-tended farms, where the Classen sisters, Elizabeth, Martha, and Mary, reunite after inheriting their family home. Together, they operate Secondhand Blessings, a charming gift-and-thrift store, housed in the old homestead's barn. Little do the sisters suspect as they stock their shelves with Amish handcrafted gift items, antiques, and yummy baked goods that they're also filling their rustic store with a host of mysteries and surprises. Learn More

Reader Favorite

Mysteries of Martha's Vineyard

On the historic island of Martha's Vineyard, Massachusetts, recent widow Priscilla Latham Grant inherits a lighthouse. She's no sooner settled into her new surrounding than she comes face-to-face with wave after wave of adventure—which include rediscovered family, new friends, old homes, and head-scratching mysteries that crop up with surprising regularity. Learn More

From Our Editors

Tearoom Mysteries

Take a picturesque New England town... add some hidden treasures... a few suspicious characters... and a good measure of faith and friendship and you've brewed up Tearoom Mysteries!

Come explore at your leisure this charming village with its lovely mountain lake surrounded by wild blueberry bushes. Just like the people who come to Elaine and Jan's tearoom, you'll find yourself feeling relaxed. Learn More

A perfect blend of faith, family and fun!

You'll get sneak peeks of new releases, recommendations from other Guideposts readers, and special offers just for you . . .
and it's FREE!

Just go to Guideposts.org/Newsletters today to sign up.

Guideposts®

Visit Guideposts.org/Shop or call (800) 932-2145

Find more inspiring fiction in these best-loved Guideposts series!

Tearoom Mysteries Series

Mix one stately Victorian home, a charming lakeside town in Maine, and two adventurous cousins with a passion for tea and hospitality. Add a large scoop of intriguing mystery and sprinkle generously with faith, family, and friends, and you have the recipe for *Tearoom Mysteries.*

Sugarcreek Amish Mysteries

Be intrigued by the suspense and joyful "aha" moments in these delightful stories. Each book in the series brings together two women of vastly different backgrounds and traditions, who realize there's much more to the "simple life" than meets the eye.

Mysteries of Martha's Vineyard

What does Priscilla Latham Grant, a Kansas farm girl know about hidden treasure and rising tides, maritime history and local isle lore? Not much—but to save her lighthouse and family reputation, she better learn quickly!

Mysteries of Silver Peak

Escape to the historic mining town of Silver Peak, Colorado, and discover how one woman's love of antiques helps her solve mysteries buried deep in the town's checkered past.

**To learn more about these books,
visit Guideposts.org/Shop**